ADMIRING HIS OMEGA

C.W. GRAY

CONTENTS

✿ Created with Vellum

ACKNOWLEDGMENTS

Thank you to all the readers who enjoy my books. I love these stories and am overjoyed that there are others who love them too. I would also like to thank my patrons on Patreon. You have helped to motivate and keep me going. Finally, I also especially want to thank my favorite brainstorm buddy, Monique. Thank you for talking plot with me. You definitely fuel my creativity. Enjoy Cain and Mal's story!

CHAPTER 1

"Welcome to another episode of *Simply Living*." Malcolm Reed smiled at the camera attached to the top corner cabinet of his kitchen. "Today, I have two lovely assistants."

Van smiled widely, cheeks dimpling, and hip-bumped him. "Hello. I'm Vanessa and this is my daughter Bianca. We're keeping an eye on this terror today."

Mal gasped dramatically, pressing his hand to his heart. "Terror? Me?"

Bianca chuckled, then smiled shyly at the main camera. The sixteen-year-old was very self-conscious, and Mal thought being part of his show might help boost her confidence. His viewers were generally good-natured and fun.

"You are a troublemaker for sure," Van continued, rolling her eyes. "Now, what are we making?"

"Oh, right." Mal bounced on the tips of his feet. "So, it's April here in Maine, and the weather conditions were perfect for one of my favorite pastimes – mushroom foraging. By now you all know I'm a mycophile." He wrapped an arm around Bianca's shoulders. "Usually foraging here in the spring is tricky, but yesterday, my youngest assistant spotted the biggest patch of morel mushrooms that I've ever seen."

Bianca flushed and the freckles on her pale cheeks stood out even more. "We, umm, we're in central Maine and just got a really good rain. Mal told me that the soil has to be super wet and at least a little warm for mushrooms to grow. This year's spring has been much warmer than usual."

"She's my precious, little budding mycophile. Best assistant ever, right?" Mal smirked.

"Hey, I cleaned the mushrooms," Van protested.

Mal laughed. "Yeah, yeah. The easiest job." He stuck his tongue out at her, then looked back at the camera. "We have fresh, hand-gathered morels, so today we're going to make a simple morel studded pasta. It's both vegetarian and easy to make." He gestured around the small kitchen of his fifth wheel camper. "RV living doesn't mean you have to limit yourself to outdoor grilling. We have a full kitchen here, just a little less space, so it's just as easy to cook from scratch using fresh ingredients as it is to toss hotdogs on a grill."

"*Easy* he says," Van said, snorting. "Boy, you're delusional."

Mal shrugged. "It does take more planning, but your tummy will thank you. Fresh ingredients generally taste better and are healthier. Don't limit yourself just because you have less space and appliances. Plus, if you think about it, part of the joy of choosing the RV lifestyle is so you can explore and find interesting places. Over the past five years, I've found so many little gems. One such place here in Hobson Hills, Maine, is a cute little store called Farm Fresh."

"I love it there," Bianca said, tucking a strand of curly brown hair behind her ear. "The whole place smells like baking bread, and they sell fresh veggies and fruit."

"It's really a good place," Mal agreed. "Good prices too, which is always welcome. Yesterday, I bought so many delicious ingredients. Here's fresh butter and heavy cream – they even have a picture of the cow it came from on their packaging." He grinned. "Her name is Pooka, by the way."

"They do have the freshest and tastiest veggies there," Van said, holding up a cutting board. "Here's some freshly minced garlic and shallots that Mal bought as well."

"The pasta we'll use is some of the garganelli I made and froze from three episodes ago." Mal gave Bianca an encouraging look.

She cleared her throat nervously, then listed out the other ingredients for the dish they were making while Van and Mal smiled proudly.

The show went on as they bantered back and forth, and Bianca slowly loosened up, smiling and laughing freely.

The girl and her mom had a special place in Mal's heart. He had spent the past five summers in Hobson Hills' RV Park, close to the small house that Van and Bianca lived in. Van quickly became a good friend, and Bianca felt like his daughter from another life.

A long-haired, grey tabby with one eye jumped onto the counter and Bianca blocked him from the stove. "No, Truffle. We're the assistants today."

Mal's cat meowed loudly and gave them a dark look before hopping back to the floor.

"Yes," Mal said, smiling sweetly. "Today's dish doesn't require any Truffle hair."

"So many of your dishes do," Van said, snickering. "Whether you like it or not.

A short time later, the episode concluded with three plates of steaming pasta. Mal cut off the cameras and urged Van and Bianca to take the two seats at the small bench table separating the kitchen from the living area. His RV had a simple floorplan – living area in the middle, a step up to the kitchen on the right, and a step up to a bathroom and bedroom on the left.

"You two did so well," he said, sprawling on his small couch. Truffle instantly jumped up and settled on his lap. "Thank you for helping out today."

"No problem," Van said, mumbling around a mouth of food.

Bianca snickered. "What Mom means to say is 'thank you for the free dinner.' This is so much better than anything we make at home."

"I swear it's on par with Reuben's cooking at the pub." Van took another bite, a look of bliss covering her face.

"Is that really possible?" he asked, serious. Hobson Hills had a local pub called The Irish Rose. The place was known for its delicious food and the fresh draft beer it served, brewed by a local man.

"You only barely compare," Van answered him, shrugging. "You don't cook with meat very often, so that detracts from your score."

"I cook with fish a lot."

"Only when you catch it."

He wrinkled his nose. "Meat in stores tastes funny. Buying fresh or catching it yourself is so much better."

Van shook her head. "That's called picky eating."

"It's just simple living."

"Simple living, my ass. If you were living simply, you'd just eat a can of ravioli instead of making your own pasta once a month."

"That's just wrong." Mal fake gagged. "Can pasta? You monster."

"Snob."

Bianca giggled. "You are so bougie, Mal. I mean look at your RV. It's huge and nicer than the apartment we first lived in. Right, Mom?"

Van nodded. "His bathroom may be bigger than that apartment's kitchen."

"Now, who's being dramatic?" he asked, glaring at his friend.

Bianca's phone pinged and she grabbed it, looking at the screen excitedly. "Oh, I have to go."

"Be careful, sweetheart," Van said, reaching up to kiss Bianca's cheek. "Do you have gas money?"

"I'm just going to Paula's, Mom." She hugged Mal. "Sorry to leave so quickly. Thank you for the delicious food."

"No problem. Have fun." He held his plate high as Truffle tried to stick his face into the pasta.

"Be home by ten and text me." Van took the last bite of her pasta. "This is so good, damn it."

"Okay." Bianca grinned and practically bounced to the door. "Have a good shift at the hospital, Mom. I'll see you when you get home."

Mal waited until Bianca closed the door behind her. "Who is Paula?" he asked Van. "What happened to Jennifer? I thought they were best friends."

"Jenn and her family moved out of state late last year. Paula is a friend she met at work."

"Okay, what's wrong with Paula?" Mal shook his head. "You look like you just sucked on a lemon."

"It's not Paula. She seems nice enough. The problem is that something's going on with Bia." Van looked tired.

"What makes you think that?"

"Well, her grades are slipping. You know how hard she has to work to keep decent grades. Lately, though, she does the bare minimum for school. I thought it was work at first, but she's been working at the grocery store part-time for over a year and hasn't had a problem with it until recently."

"Can't you just make her quit the job? I can help out if she needs some extra money."

Van gave him a hard look. "We don't take charity. Plus, she seems to really like the job. I don't know why. Eugene

Scott owns the place, and the man is a grade A bastard. But it is what it is."

"There's one of those in every town," he said, scowling. "Maybe she can get a job at one of the other shops."

"Easier said than done." She sipped her water for a moment. "The job isn't really the problem. It's just... she keeps things from me now. Bia used to tell me everything, even if I didn't want to know. Since she started hanging out with Paula, things are different. At least, that's what I tell myself."

"It can't be that bad," he said. "She has a good head on her shoulders. One teenage girl's influence isn't going to change her."

"I found condoms and underwear under her mattress," Van said bluntly. "I don't mean cotton briefs either, but lace thongs and shit like that. I didn't even know she knew where to buy that stuff, but I guess you *can* get anything online."

"No," he said, drawing the word out as he gasped. "No, no, no. Our angel isn't ready for sex. Teenage boys are irresponsible assholes. I know. I was one." He stood up. "I'm going to bring her back home right now. This Paula clearly isn't good for Bianca."

Van tossed a rolled up napkin at him. "Sit down. If we try forcing her to do anything, she'll be even more reckless. I know. I was a teenage girl too. We've talked about safe sex and what makes a good partner, but I don't know how much she's really listened. I thought my parents didn't know anything when I was her age."

"What do we do?" he asked, pacing the floor. Bianca was sweet, but so insecure. It wouldn't be hard for someone to take advantage of her. "Once, I stole my older sister's car keys before she went on a date with a guy that I thought was a vampire. It worked and kept her home, so should I steal Bianca's Vespa?"

"She would murder you. She worked so hard last summer to pay for it. Wait, why did you think the boy was a vampire?" She held her hand up before he could say anything. "Never mind, don't tell me. It might start making sense and that scares me."

Mal bit his lip hard and grabbed Truffle. He hugged the cat tightly. "I blame the Twilight movies. He was pale, and we lived in Washington."

"I said I didn't want to know, damn it." Van carried the plates to the sink. "You even have a dishwasher in your RV? Bougie, Mal. You're a bougie fucker."

"What if she isn't at Paula's?" he asked. "What if she's in the back of some guy's car right now?"

"Then I ground her for a year." She groaned. "Stop speculating. You're making me worry more. Teenagers are frustrating, Mal. Two stars. I don't recommend."

"You work a lot, Van. That, plus the long drive to and from the hospital, means she's alone a lot. Should I start following her and keep an eye on things?"

Van blinked slowly, staring at him. "Yes, a thirty-year-old, grown-ass man should follow a teen girl around town. No one will think that's creepy at all."

"I'm twenty-seven."

"That's what you take offense to?" Van shook her head. "You ain't right, Mal. Listen, we're probably worrying for nothing. Paula isn't a bad kid, and her dad is a nice man. He's a single parent too and puts in the work. You know what I mean?"

"You'll let me know if you need anything from me?" He gave her a worried look. "You two are important to me, even if I only see you three to four months a year."

"You're family, you weirdo." Van gave him a soft look and patted his cheek. "I need to get ready for work. You and your fancy dishwasher can handle clean-up, right?"

"Sure. Have a good night." He hung out the door as she walked the short distance to her house. "Call me if you need me, Van. For real!"

LATER THAT NIGHT, Mal was still worried about Bianca. He didn't know anything about raising teens, but he knew what kind of trouble they could get into. He had grown up with four siblings and a shit ton of cousins. The amount of trouble they had gotten into was staggering. Especially the quiet ones.

"It's always the quiet ones," he mumbled, adjusting the headpiece of his Chewbacca costume.

Rueben and Ernie Hart's cabin was nestled on a remote, wooded road. He had it on good authority that the two men would be at the cabin that night for some alone time.

"Sorry, Ernie, but I need to destress," he whispered and approached the window of the kitchen. The interior lights were on, so he knew they were there. He saw movement inside, and bent down, creeping slowly to the closest window.

The sound of running water suggested someone was at the kitchen sink. "Perfect."

Inch by inch, he rose up in the window, waiting eagerly for the screams of joy he was sure would come. Ernie Hart was known to be obsessed with Bigfoot. He'd likely run out and try to catch Mal. *Pranking the Wilsons is the best*, he thought giggling in happiness.

His giggles stopped instantly. Instead of Ernie, a handsome man in his mid-thirties stared at Mal through the window. The man was dressed in a slightly rumpled suit, and his dark brown hair was disheveled. His chiseled face was somber and perfectly calm. Mal was enraptured by brown eyes deep enough to drown in.

The man reached out and opened the window. "Hello?"

"Well, this is awkward," Mal said, shuffling his feet.

"You were expecting Ernie, weren't you?"

Mal nodded then sighed and took off the headpiece. "Yeah. Reuben and he were supposed to be here this weekend."

The man nodded. "You are correct. They even lined up a sitter for the children."

"So, umm, he's not here?" Mal felt like a little kid asking his friend's parent if they were home.

"No. Rueben and he lent me the cabin for a couple of days. They went to the coast for the weekend instead. I'm Cain, by the way. Cain Benson."

"Mal Reed."

"Would you like a cup of tea? I was about to have a chamomile blend. It helps with sleep." The worry lines on Cain's face told Mal the man really needed a good night's sleep.

Mal ran his hand through his hair. "I could use it, I guess. My teenage daughter-from-another-life has started dating. I really need to relax, and my yoga group couldn't get together at such short notice. Doing yoga by yourself is just not the same, you know?"

"Are you old enough to have a teenage daughter?"

"Thank you." Mal threw his hairy Chewbacca arms up. "I'm only twenty-seven. *Some* people keep trying to give me years." He made a face. "While I am young and virile, Bianca isn't mine biologically, but if I had a daughter, she would be it."

"How lovely," Cain said, the side of his mouth twitching.

"Anyway, do you do yoga?"

"I do not."

"You really should. It has so many benefits." Mal crossed his arms and leaned on the window frame. "It's my second favorite way to reduce anxiety."

Cain raised a brow and gave him an interested look. "What's your favorite way?"

"D&D," Mal answered immediately. "I have a group I've been campaigning with since junior high. We zoom every Thursday."

"That was not what I expected you to say, but alright. I will put the kettle on."

"Thanks." Mal grinned, watching the man work. He was quick and efficient, moving gracefully about the small kitchen. "Are you in Hobson Hills to visit your parents?"

"You know my parents?"

"Not really, but small towns and gossip. Am I right? I basically know everything about the Wilsons and their friends."

ain Benson eyed the cute omega in the window suspiciously. "Why do you want to know so much about the Wilsons?"

"Who wouldn't?" Mal shrugged. "Anyway, why are you in town? I thought the last Benson son was a lawyer in Georgia."

"Are small towns really this nosy?" Cain wiped his hand over his face, fighting the exhaustion that had led him to leave his work in Atlanta for a few days.

"They are." Mal nodded. "Trust me. I'm an expert on them. Hobson Hills is one of the better ones, but everyone is still happy to share their neighbor's business for a cup of coffee."

Cain sighed and walked away from the window to unlock the kitchen door. "Please, come inside and sit down. If we are going to talk, you might as well be comfortable."

Mal bounced as he walked, making Cain's lips twitch again. The omega was cute. He was tall with curly brown hair, freckles, and kind blue eyes. Those eyes were familiar, but Cain knew he had never met the other man. He would have remembered.

"Is there a reason you wanted to frighten Ernie?" Cain filled the kettle and put it on the stove, then pulled two cups from the cabinet.

"I don't want to scare him." Mal plopped in a chair at the small kitchen table. "Ernie loves Bigfoot, so a close encounter will make him happy. Well, until he realizes I'm not Bigfoot. Anyway, pranking one of the Wilsons is just a bit of silly. Like when I put scary faces and arms on some of Elijah's apple trees in his orchard or when I switched around the plants in Janelle's greenhouse. All harmless, I swear."

"Elijah is a Benson now," Cain corrected, fighting a laugh. This man was an odd one for sure.

"Nope. Once a Wilson, always a Wilson." Mal's eyes twinkled with mischief. "You're close to being one too."

"Are you teasing me?" Cain arched a brow.

Mal arched his own brow. "Do you have to ask?"

Cain snorted as he laughed.

The omega propped his chin on his fist. "Are you going to tell me what brought you to town now? Pretty, pretty please?"

"I suppose I can." Cain took his time making the tea, relishing the tap, tap, tap of Mal's foot. The omega was so impatient. "Here, drink up."

"Cain Benson, big time lawyer from Atlanta," Mal said, eyes narrowing. "Spill the tea, handsome."

Cain laughed. "There is no drama here. I missed my family. That's all."

The omega's gentle blue eyes darkened with sadness. "That's fair. Atlanta is a long way away."

Cain found the ever-present tension in his shoulders easing. "When I'm working, I'm fine, but I cannot work all the time."

"It's the quiet moments, when you're alone that are the worst, right?" Mal gave him a sympathetic look.

Cain nodded. "My apartment is too quiet. I miss all my nieces and nephews."

"Didn't Yeo just have another kid?"

"He did. Robin." Cain smiled softly as he thought of his newest nephew. "A few months after, Yeo and Caden accidently got pregnant again."

"Shit! That's nine nieces and nephews for you." Mal seemed pleased. "I love it."

"It makes me nervous that you know that." Cain eyed the man suspiciously.

"Don't worry about it." Mal waved a hand, completely unconcerned. "Everyone in town probably keeps count. How is the newest doing?"

Cain couldn't help but smile as he thought of Robin. "Each and every one of them is astounding, but Robin is the squishiest, cutest one of them all."

Mal grinned. "Aww, you're so sweet. I don't have any nieces or nephews yet, but some of my cousins have kids, and they're a handful. I think the Wilsons are even more chaotic, so your holidays must be wild. It's probably nice though."

"Sometimes." Cain sipped his tea. "Why are you so interested in the Wilsons?"

"No nefarious reason." Mal shrugged.

Cain gave him a considering look. "You know more about me, than I know about you. I don't like it."

"I'm not so sure about that." Mal leaned on the table. "You know that I'm young and virile, have a surrogate daughter, and enjoy pranking the Wilsons. That's a lot if you think about it."

Cain forced himself to keep a straight face. "Where are you from?"

"A small town in Washington. Lots of family." Mal snorted. "Too much family really. My family tree is more like a forest of trees connected together with strings of flashing lights and windchimes. Loud, obnoxious windchimes."

"That sounds… lovely." Cain pressed his lips together, then asked, "What town?"

Mal tsked. "You want the details too?"

Cain arched his brow and struggled not to smile when Mal made a face. The omega was simply too easy to read.

"Tiny place called Thorn Creek," Mal said, then sipped his tea. "Most of my immediate and extended family live there."

"Do you miss them?"

Mal looked conflicted. "Yes, but it's complicated." He shook himself and grinned at Cain, wagging his eyebrows. "At the moment, I'd rather live the life of a rambling man."

Cain's lips twitched again. "A rambling man?"

"I have a RV and travel all over the US and Canada." Mal leaned back in his chair, smirking. "I'm a loner, never staying in one place. A nonconforming maverick. The ultimate free spirit."

Cain tapped his chin and tilted his head to the side. "Why do I not believe you?"

Mal gave him a disappointed look. "I *could* be a mysterious rogue on the run from a dark past. You don't know me."

"Are you a writer?"

Mal chuckled, looking delighted. "I wish. No, I'm a vlogger."

"Is that a real profession?" Cain frowned. "How do you make money?"

Mal sniffed and gave him a wounded look. "I make enough to get by, thank you very much. More importantly, you should ask me what I post about."

"Please, forgive me, mysterious traveling vlogger," Cain

said, voice tinged with laughter despite his efforts. "What do you post about?"

Mal's expression brightened and Cain swore the whole room became lighter and more cheerful. "I post about a lot of different things, but my most profitable content is about cooking from scratch. I film short episodes, edit them, and post to multiple places. I even have sponsors now."

"Interesting. How would I find your work?"

"My site is called *Simply Living*." Mal cupped his tea in both furry hands. "It's really starting to take off. Basically, I focus on getting back to the basics with food and life. I choose recipes that use a minimal amount of natural ingredients but still taste yummy. Since I travel so much, I do episodes about finding the best places to buy fresh ingredients and where to forage when it's legal. I'm well known in the mycophile community," he stated proudly. "Do you think Ernie would give me permission to hunt mushrooms out here? I saw some prime spots when I was sneaking in."

"Wow, you sound so mysterious, you scoundrel," Cain said dryly, rubbing his chin. "Can I trust a wild mycophile around my friends?"

Mal gave him a wounded look. "How could you ask such a thing? I may be the bad boy of mushroom foraging, but I forage for good, not evil. I'm completely trustworthy."

Cain chose to ignore the fact that he had caught Mal trespassing mere moments ago. "Ernie and Reuban probably won't mind but ask them first. Get the permission in writing if possible."

"Okay, Mr. Lawyer."

"Do you really make money doing all that? Foraging and whatnot?"

Mal shrugged. "Enough to pay most of my bills. I started it as a hobby, but it really hit with a lot of people. Oh, I also have a beginner's yoga channel. It's not as popular as my cooking one, but you should join it. Yoga would really help with your stress."

"I look that stressed?"

Mal nodded. "The bags under your eyes have stories to tell. You don't just miss your family, do you?"

Cain pressed his lips together, wincing. "No."

"Do you want to talk about it?" Mal reached across the table and settled his fur covered hand on Cain's. "You gave me free legal advice after all."

Cain shook his head. "It makes me feel pathetic." It was unlike him to even consider telling someone something so personal. Mal was really a stranger and had admitted to liking gossip. It would be stupid to tell him anything important.

"We're friends now, right? Please tell me?" Mal pouted and stared at him with the best puppy eyes that Cain had ever come across in an adult. "I'll tell you my secrets too."

"Fine." Cain drew the word out as he sighed in defeat. "I want a family of my own. A partner and a child."

"Hmm. That's not exactly surprising. Human beings are social after all." Mal looked puzzled. "You're handsome, have a job, and seem like a nice enough man. Why don't you already have a partner?"

Cain gave the omega a flat look. "That is the question my mother asks me every time she calls."

Mal snickered, then looked guilty. "I'm sorry. That was rude. So, really. What's the problem? If you aren't interested in omegas, your parents would understand. Surely you know that. Oh, wait. Are you extra kinky? There are communities for that and you shouldn't feel ashamed."

Cain felt his face heat. "Please stop talking. It isn't anything like that."

Mal looked doubtful. "It's alright. Really, there's no shame in loving someone."

"Oh, shut up. I simply haven't found anyone I want to be with." Cain scowled. "I've dated many people. It's not like I'm not looking. I've met some amazing omegas. They came from a similar economic background and were handsome, well-mannered, and highly intelligent. Each one was an admirable person with many good qualities." Cain winced. "It just doesn't feel right with them."

"Admirable, huh? Well, maybe you're trying too hard." Mal shrugged. "One of my older cousins went years dating anyone she could because she wanted a family more than anything, then when she finally gave up on meeting the right person, she realized she really liked her next-door neighbor. They've been married three years now."

"Lucky for her," Cain said, grimacing. "No, it's just that there *is* one man, but it's impossible."

"Unrequited love?" Mal gave him a sympathetic look. "I'm very familiar with that."

"Not love." Cain's face flushed. "Not yet. It could be though. Call it an intense case of like. No one else stands a chance as long as I'm around him."

"Why is it impossible? Life can really surprise you. For example, one of my other cousins always wanted to be an artist, but he gave up on that idea since it seemed too far-fetched. He became a nurse instead. Then, years later, his art started to sell. He just recently quit his job at the hospital and started painting full time."

"How many cousins do you have? Never mind. It really is impossible. Besides the fact that he's a good friend, he's in a loving relationship *and* he's currently an employee. There are many reasons he isn't a good choice for me." Cain shook his head. "No, I think it will be best for me to leave Atlanta all together."

"I completely understand." Mal leaned forward. "Do you

want to go on the road with me? My couch pulls out into a bed."

Despite the heavy conversation, Cain struggled not to laugh. This omega was completely ridiculous. They had only just met. "As tempting as that sounds, I plan to move to Hobson Hills permanently. I'm not happy with my life in Atlanta, so I will build a new one here. Hopefully with someone fitting."

Mal clapped happily. "Yes! Good. Your brothers and parents will really like that. Personally, I think your dad misses you the most. He's always bragging about you and gets excited when you come by to visit."

"It really does worry me that you know us well enough to say that." Cain drank the last of his tea. "Now, you promised to tell me your story."

"Oh, yeah." Mal narrowed his eyes. "You promise you won't tell anyone what I'm about to say?"

"Did you break any laws?" Cain felt it was prudent to ask before he promised to keep quiet.

"None that were important."

"All laws are important." Cain rubbed his face again and sighed. "Why do I feel like you won't listen to me anyway? Fine. I promise I won't tell anyone what you say."

"You and I have a lot in common." Mal gave him a dramatically sad look. "It was a classic cliché for me. I fell in love with my straight best friend. He fell for one of my younger cousins. They're married now. I'm a godparent to their daughter. Woe is me. I shall never be happy again."

Cain studied the omega. Mal seemed to want to laugh it off, but Cain could sense some real pain behind the smiles. In situations like this, there were no villains to blame. No one to take your anger out on. People couldn't help how they felt. "Was it really love?"

Mal nodded. "Oh yeah. Took years for it to grow, but it was rooted deep."

"Do they live in Thorn Creek?"

"Yep." Mal took a swig of his tea. "I see them any time I go home." He shrugged. "Trina is family, and Rick and I still stay in touch. He's in my D&D group and we talk all the time. There's too much friendship there to just cut him out of my life. It's not his fault I fell in love with him. That was all me."

"Is that why you're here instead of in Washington?"

"It's why I left, but now I'm where I want to be." Mal smiled wryly. "Rick and I created this game app in college that became popular. He did the coding; I did the design. We had more in the works, and it could have turned into something big. Our families thought we'd start a business together. Our paths were set."

"What happened?"

"Rick started dating Trina, and I decided I wanted out. We sold the app, made a bit of money, and I bought my RV and hit the road. I always wanted to come to Hobson Hills, so this was one of the destinations on my map."

"Why Hobson Hills?" Cain asked, baffled. "How did you even know it existed?"

Mal avoided his gaze. "A family member mentioned it. Anyway, that's my sad story. I was forced into a nomadic lifestyle because of unrequited love."

"Does it help?" Cain asked, voice soft. "Being far away?"

A variety of emotions played across the omega's face. "At first, it was absolutely necessary. It was exhausting seeing them together all the time and having to act like everything was great. Now, though, it's just convenient. Being physically distant doesn't mean we're not close. It just let me set my boundaries and heal. I think I'll always love him a little, but after five years of being apart, that affection doesn't control my life anymore. I can move on."

"I really like that." Being around Jasper wasn't torture for Cain, but it wasn't pleasant. He didn't want to imagine being in a position like Mal's, and if he stayed right where he was in Atlanta, Cain knew the situation would get worse. "Do you think you'll fall in love again?" he asked.

"I sure hope so." Mal grinned. "Unrequited love sucks, but I've seen love work too. But that's not my whole life. I like who I am now. I'm happy without being one half of a whole."

"Do the tricks help keep you happy?" Cain asked. "Would pranking Ernie really help you feel better?"

Mal met his gaze, puppy eyes pleading. "It feeds my soul."

"He has a trail camera set up behind the house." Cain stood and pulled Mal to his feet. "He checks it every other day. You should take off the ammo belt. While it is true to Chewie, you will resemble a sasquatch more without it."

Mal grinned and the room brightened again. "I think I could fall in love with you, Cain Benson."

"You are far too easy to impress. Come along. I fly out in the morning, so if Ernie checks the camera and sees a sasquatch running off with me, he will believe it for a while."

Mal ran for the door. "You are seriously the best person in the whole world. I will cook for you anytime you want, Benson. Anytime. Do you think I can carry you on my shoulder? I have a strong core. You are so joining my yoga group now. What times work well for you?"

Cain sighed and closed his eyes, wondering where he had gone wrong.

CHAPTER 3

"Thank you, Mr. Hart," Mal said as he folded the signed agreement and slid it into his pocket. "I'll share if I find any good spots."

Reuben gave him a brisk nod, clearly uncomfortable to be speaking to a stranger. The large man usually let his husband do the talking for him, but Ernie was busy.

"Are you sure he's alright?" Ernie asked, pacing the floor as he talked on the phone. He carried one of the couple's young children in his arms while the other two watched from their play area. "The footage was clear as day. Bigfoot got him, Carter. He carried poor Cain away."

Reuben rolled his eyes and Mal fought not to laugh. *Best prank ever*, he thought.

"Yes, that was Bigfoot." Ernie stopped pacing and stomped his foot like a toddler. "Carter, I know what I saw. You need to interview Cain about the encounter. He may know where Bigfoot is now." He paused for a moment. "Carter Benson, if you've ever cared for our friendship at all you will facetime your brother and ask him where Bigfoot is."

"Carter Benson," the toddler in Ernie's arms called out, waving an arm in outrage.

"Carter Benson," the other toddler called from the play area, giggling.

The youngest ignored his two older siblings and leaned against the large husky lying next to them.

"Do you hear that?" Ernie asked, smug. "The twins are in full agreement with me. You know your job, Carter. Do it now and report back to me."

"Please, ignore him," Reuben said, deep voice full of laughter.

"That is impossible, and you know it. Anyway, I'll get going." Mal smiled sweetly. "Nice meeting you. I'll tell everyone I see about Ernie's tantrum, but you probably know that too."

Reuben sighed and nodded.

"Have a good day." Mal hurried toward the truck, cackling.

"What did you do in there?" Bianca asked him when he climbed in. Her curly brown hair was pulled into a messy bun on the top of her head. She was dressed cozy in an over-sized sweater and leggings. The weather had turned again a few days ago, and the air was a little too crisp for Mal's comfort. He wished he had brought a sweater too.

"Why do you think I did something?" he asked, turning up the heat.

"It's the smile." She sighed and shook her head. "Plus, you made me go put baby bonnets on alpacas while you were inside. Why do you enjoy teasing the Wilsons so much?"

He shrugged. "It brings me joy. So, what do you want to do today?"

"Try to take over the world," she replied in a solemn voice.

Mal laughed. "Oh, I do love you."

"I'm glad to hear that because I made plans for us."

"How mysterious." He wiggled his brows. "What are we doing?"

One of his favorite things about visiting Hobson Hills was spending time with Bianca. Van worked a lot, so Mal and Bianca were left to their own devices most of the time when she wasn't in school or working.

The teenager cleared her throat and pulled out her phone. "First, we'll have breakfast at Honey Buns in town."

"Coffee and pastries." He nodded. "I approve."

"Then, we'll stop at the bookstore so I can pick up a graphic novel I ordered."

"Nice. Supporting small businesses."

"Of course." Bianca gave him a curt nod. "Then, after that, we'll go to the thrift store to look for decorative fruit and veggies. When the Wilsons' gardens start growing this year, we'll trade the plastic ones for a few of the real ones. That should be a surprise, right? We can hit most of them in one night."

He stared at her for a moment, amazed at the angel beside him. "I'm so proud of you. Van and I raised you right."

She grinned. "After the thrift store, we'll go to the animal sanctuary outside of town. There's someone I want you to meet."

"Person or animal?" he asked.

"Animal."

"I'll allow it."

"Then, since it's raining, we'll go back to your RV and binge *What We Do in the Shadows*."

"You'll finally watch my favorite show?" He narrowed his eyes and gave her a quick look as he backed out of Ernie and Reuben's driveway. "Wait, why are we doing so many things I like? Are you secretly taking me to the dentist or something? Oh god, do you have bad news to give me? Is Van dying?"

Bianca shook her head. "No, I just missed you."

"Damn it, kid. I missed you too."

"Plus, I invited Paula and her dad to dinner at the RV tonight. He wants to meet you before he'll let Paula come mushroom hunting with us. Can you make your vegetarian enchiladas? Paula swears they sound gross, but I know she'll love them."

"Aha! That's what you're really after."

Bianca laughed. "I really did miss you. I figure you and I are going to hang a lot this summer, and I'll want Paula to come sometimes. This way, her dad can get to know you."

"Does your friend really want to forage with us?" he asked. "Not that I doubt how awesome we are, but not everyone is a mycophile like us."

Bianca snorted. "Seriously. I don't understand why, but she wants to come with us. Likes nature and all that."

"Alright," he said, still feeling doubtful. "Your mom will be home for dinner too, so I'll need to cook for five. Six if Cain stops by."

Mal's new friend was back in town for the weekend and had promised to come by when he was able. It had only been a week since they'd met, but Mal was already eager to see him again.

"Cain?"

"A friend."

"A friend?" Bianca looked interested. "What kind of friend?"

"The kind that lets me carry him over my shoulder while I'm dressed like Chewbacca."

"TMI." She squeezed her eyes shut and looked like she was about to throw up. "I don't need to know about your sex life."

He laughed, not bothering to correct her. "I'll plan for six."

"Homemade tortillas?" Bianca asked hopefully, eyes still closed.

"Who do you think I am?" He scoffed. "Of course, we'll use homemade tortillas." He eyed her again. "If you tell me who you're dating."

She smirked. "What a shame. You already taught me how to make the tortillas myself. Guess I'll have to make them."

AN HOUR LATER, Mal savored his third cup of coffee, practically vibrating in place, as he stared down at the sow and piglets in front of him. Bianca knelt in the straw and pet one of the piglets.

Teague, the owner of the sanctuary, watched them from outside the stall. "A hobby farmer a few towns over passed away. He had no family, so the state surrendered his animals here. This is one of six Kunekune pigs he had. Fortunately, she was the only pregnant one. Her name is Daisy. The piglets are weaned and ready to find their forever homes."

"Six? Why was he raising so many of them?"

"For meat," Teague answered, shrugging. "They're easier to handle then larger breeds."

Mal winced. "Poor piggies."

"Bacon comes from somewhere." Teague smiled innocently when Mal glared at him.

"Pigs are really smart," Bianca said, looking at him hopefully. "You could save one from becoming bacon by training her to search for truffles."

"I'm sure these piggies aren't going to become bacon. Plus, Maine doesn't really have the right weather for truffles to grow."

"Train her to search for mushrooms then. That would be a big help, right? You could find a lot more in a shorter amount of time."

"I live in an RV," Mal said, laughing.

"That's okay." Bianca waved his concerns away. "Betty could stay with me when you're not in Hobson Hills. We have a big yard. Teague said he would help me create an area for her to live in."

"Betty?"

Bianca smiled sweetly and held a small, tricolor piglet up. "This is Betty. She's very smart. She's already leash trained. I'm sure we could train her to find mushrooms in no time. She would be a working girl, so she'll pay for herself."

"What does your mom think about this?" he asked, arching a brow. He seriously doubted Van wanted a pet when she was always away from home.

"She said that if I could convince you to adopt Betty, she'd buy a sidecar for my Vespa and clean the bathroom for a year. She obviously wants Betty."

He snorted. "You mean she said, 'If you manage to convince Mal to adopt a pig, I'll buy you that sidecar you've been wanting and clean the bathroom for a whole year. Ha ha ha. Sarcastic tone, blah, blah, blah.'"

Bianca gave him an innocent look. "That's basically what I said, right?"

Van clearly underestimated what he would do for Bianca. "What's the adoption process?"

Teague's smile resembled that of a shark. "Come to my office and we'll start the paperwork. Note Daisy's size. Piglets don't stay tiny forever. I'll show you the daddy pig too. The enclosure I'll help Bianca build will be good for her, but she'll need a lot of attention. Bianca says you spend most of your time outdoors and will take Betty with you. Is that accurate?"

"Yes." He sighed. "Truffle is going to be mad at me."

"Truffle?"

"My cat."

Teague snorted. "Truffle the cat? I like it. That means there's at least one truffle in Maine. These pigs are already used to cats, so there shouldn't be a problem on Betty's end."

"Truffle likes other animals too." Mal bent and scratched under the piglet's chin. Kunekune pigs were hairy and had the cutest, forward-facing ears. Betty's coat was a silky mix of black, white, and brown.

"It won't all be on you either. Bianca and Van have both been volunteering here since we opened. I trust that they'll take good care of Betty when you're out of town. Don't let them fool you. They have been planning on adopting a pet for a while. Bianca clearly picked Betty with you in mind, but she's ready for a full-time pet."

"See? I'm not *that* bad, Mal." Bianca laughed and took his coffee cup so she could hand him the piglet. "I really think you'll like her though."

Teague patted his shoulder. "I'm sure she'll be a valuable truffle pig in no time."

"Maine doesn't have non-cat truffles." Mal grumbled and climbed out of the stall to follow the other man, Betty held safely in his arms. "Damn, I need another coffee."

A FEW HOURS LATER, Bianca and Paula sat on his sofa with Truffle the cat, eyes glued to the television. Instead of *What They Do in the Shadows*, a reality show was on. It was for the best, though. Once he started watching his favorite show, he couldn't stop.

Paula's dad, Mark, sat at the table, chopping and deseeding peppers while Cain stood at a counter, carefully cutting baby bella mushrooms. Both men had arrived at Mal's at the same time and seemed to get on well.

"There are a lot of houses for sale close to the lake where your parents live." Mark glanced at Cain over his shoulder. "If you want, I can line some up for you to view. No pressure, though."

"I haven't told anyone else I'm moving here yet," Cain said. "Can you keep it on the down low?"

"Absolutely. I'll leave you my card and you can email me when you're ready."

Cain gave Mal a look. "I hadn't realized I would get to talk to a realtor tonight."

"Serendipitous." Mal stirred the enchilada sauce, then flipped the tortillas in the skillet. The kitchen was a mess from rolling out the dough, but it smelled deliciously spicy. The girls had already extended the RV's canopy and set the outdoor table up. The rain still fell but the outdoor curtains and small patio heater he'd pulled out of storage kept the space cozy. For the first time in years, Mal regretted not having a dining room. He also wasn't sure he had enough plates but figured he could borrow some from Van if they needed more.

Betty danced around his feet, grunting softly. The piglet had completely abandoned Bianca in favor of Mal. He blamed it on the bits of food he occasionally dropped while cooking, but Bianca was convinced Mal and Betty were soulmates.

"By the way, Carter called me again this morning to ask who was on Ernie's trail cam." Cain scooped up mushroom slices and placed them in a bowl. "Do you know how hard it is to dodge his questions? He even had Mom call me."

Mark's eyes rounded comically. "Please tell me that was you, Mal. Ernie has been telling everyone who will listen about Bigfoot carrying Cain Benson off to his lair. The video's been uploaded to the town's community board. Ernie wants to create a Bigfoot festival for next year."

Mal cackled evilly. "Best. Prank. Ever."

"Okay, I'll trust Van's taste in found family." Mark nodded. "You may take my daughter mushroom hunting."

"Another mycophile?" Cain asked, shaking his head. "You're a bad influence, Mal. What will the younger generation become?"

Betty nibbled on Mal's toes, her short nose tickling his bare feet and making him giggle. "Betty, really. Will you stop that?"

"Where did the pig come from anyway?" Cain asked, tossing Betty a small piece of mushroom. "I thought you only had a cat."

"The daughter of my heart decided we needed a truffle pig."

Mark and Cain both eyed Betty doubtfully.

"Hey, I can train her," Mal said defensively. "Bia ensures me that Betty is very smart."

The two men quietly watched Betty zoom in circles around Mal.

"Are you sure?" Cain asked, wincing when Betty tripped and rolled a couple of times before jumping back up to continue circling her favorite person.

"Eh, at least she's cute." Mal shrugged and removed the last tortilla from the skillet. Bianca was supposed to be doing this part, but she looked so happy sitting with her friend. "Am I the soft parent?"

The door opened suddenly, banging against the wall and startling everyone. Van looked around wildly before her eyes settled on Betty. "Damn you, Mal. I can't believe you let her get the pig. I have to buy her a freaking sidecar now."

"And clean the bathroom for a year," Bianca called out from the couch, attention still on the television. "Love you, Mom."

"Yes," Cain answered promptly. "You are definitely the soft parent."

CHAPTER 4

Cain stayed with Mal after dinner to clean up. That was all it was. He was just helping a friend clean up since he had cooked dinner for everyone. While he was at it, he told himself that he had taken another weekend off and flown over a thousand miles just to visit his parents again. It was absolutely not because he wanted to see Mal.

Betty and Truffle lay together on a new pet bed next to the couch while their human hummed a tune as he danced around the small kitchen, wiping already clean counters one more time. Outside of a Chewbacca costume, the man went from cute to dangerously handsome with a tall, slender, firm frame. Cain had known Mal had long lashes and expressive, plump lips, but hadn't known his everyday look included a bit of eyeliner and delicate jewelry. It amazed the alpha that Mal could go from ruffled hair and freckles to styled and sexy so easily. He also clearly looked happy in the kitchen, even a small one like the RV's.

"You like cooking for people." Cain started the dishwasher, then leaned on the tiny island in the center of the room.

"I forgot how much I enjoy it," Mal admitted, smiling sheepishly. "I used to cook for my cousins all the time. Everyone in my age group would get together for dinner once a month to catch up. It's been a while since I cooked for more than myself. I make friends everywhere I go, but not like this. Even crowded, it was fun, wasn't it?"

Cain nodded. "I like your daughter from another life. I also find it highly enjoyable when Van puts you in a head-lock. What did you think about Paula? That was the girl you were worried about, right?"

Mal huffed, frustrated. "She seemed nice, damn it. I don't think I can blame her for Bianca keeping secrets. My favorite teenager in the whole dang world wouldn't tell me who she was dating either. She wouldn't even admit to seeing anyone."

Cain winced.

"Yeah." Mal nodded his head. "Exactly. Anyway, are you really going to start looking for a house?"

"I think so. I have a few problems I need to take care of first, but it wouldn't hurt to go ahead and have a place set up here."

Mal went to the couch and lifted a cushion. He pulled a notebook out from under it and handed it to Cain. "There's a pen stuck to the fridge. Write down what you're looking for in a home. I bet you like lists."

"I do." Cain also liked that Mal called his future house a home. "A big kitchen so you'll come cook for me again," he began. "At least three bedrooms and two bathrooms. I want it on the lake. Dad swears I'll enjoy fishing if I ever give it a try."

"You've never been fishing?" Mal gave him a sympathetic look. "You poor thing."

Cain raised a brow. It was hard to picture the sexy man next to him in a fly hat and waders.

"A small yard," he continued. "I don't want to have to take care of acres of land." Cain eyed Betty and Truffle. "Maybe a slightly larger yard. The pet to person ratio in Hobson Hills is rather high. You were even conned into a pet."

Mal laughed. "Yeah, one I'm not at all equipped to handle. I haven't had a dog in a while, little less a pig. Do you know how many puddles I've had to clean up so far today? How do you potty train a pig?"

"Didn't Bianca say she'd take over once the enclosure is built?"

"Yes, but I'll miss Betty if she stays with them overnight. I want to keep my little cutie here with me."

Cain rolled his eyes. "You were easy to con, weren't you?"

"Way too easy." Mal pulled him to the couch, and they sat down. "Keep going and write this down so you can send it to Mark. Are three bedrooms enough? You said you want kids. Is this your forever home or something temporary until you meet your one true love?"

"One true love?" Cain scoffed. A moment later his lips lifted unconsciously. "A forever home, though? I like that."

"One day, I'll be ready for one of mine own too. It's important to think these things out." Mal tapped the notebook. "How many kids?"

"Two?"

"Are you asking me or telling me?"

"Two," Cain said, more certain this time.

"Then you should try for four or five bedrooms, depending on your budget. You Bensons have family money, so it's worth it to invest in your home sooner rather than later."

"You know our finances too?" Cain leaned his head against the back cushions and closed his eyes. "Here, you take the notes. Add on there that I need to do a background check on you."

"I'll text you a reminder next week if you join one of my yoga groups. I promise, it will help you relax."

Cain kept his eyes closed and fought a laugh. "Deal. I suppose the house should have four bedrooms."

"Good thinking. Now, about the kitchen. It should have a nice view for when you're washing dishes. Plenty of cabinet space, of course. Oh, and an island with seating so your friends can keep you company while you cook."

"Sure." Cain didn't have the heart to tell Mal that he never cooked.

Mal poked him with the pencil. "Hey, are you trying to go to sleep? Do you not get any rest in Atlanta? You need to move quickly. What do you still need to do in Atlanta before you can leave?"

Cain opened his eyes and scowled at the thought of what waited for him back home. "A friend of mine is having some trouble."

"The man you love?"

"No, my best friend Roe. And I don't *love* Jasper. Not yet."

"Jasper." Mal mulled over the name. "Is he one of those *admirable* omegas you talked about? Is that why you could fall in love with him given the chance?"

"Why don't you like the word *admirable*?"

Mal made a face. "It's just a weird way to describe someone you're romantically interested in. It sounds like they must be worthy of your attention to keep your interest. People have flaws, and if you put them on a pedestal, you *will* be disappointed. No one fits in a box, Cain. Each person is an assortment of memories, genetics, and emotions. Think multifaceted. Like mushrooms. You can steam, sauté, grill, and bake them."

Cain thought about what Mal was saying. "Jasper *is* multifaceted. He came from a lower socioeconomic background than I did which gives him a perspective I lack. He's intelligent, career driven, and presents himself well, as expected of someone representing our firm. It's been in my family for generations and the Bensons are well known to other prominent families in the area. He's taken to attending all the networking events. People like him."

Mal wrinkled his nose. "Hmm."

"Hmm?" Cain fought a smile.

"Does that mean that you like him because he fits in with your rich family friends despite coming from a less *prominent* family?"

"I don't think so." Cain frowned. "I suppose I like him because he *doesn't* quite fit in with them. When he first began attending the networking events, they treated him poorly. As if he was a pity hire. However, he stood up for himself and won't let them push him around. It's not only that, though. Jasper does the same thing for his clients, no matter who they are. He also has a knack for finding the clients that need him the most, and he moves mountains to help them. I believe I admire him because his priority is helping those who need it rather than making money."

"Hmm," Mal tapped his chin. "Okay, I may have a crush on Jasper too. He sounds like a badass."

Cain laughed, surprised at himself. Mal had a way of making him smile even as he forced Cain to think about all the complex, muddled feelings inside of him. "Well, he's taken. His fiancée is a good person, and they are disgustingly in love with one another."

"Oh, well." Mal shrugged. "I'll have to find another crush to *admire*. Hey, aren't you a lawyer too? Don't you fight for the innocent?"

"Presumed innocent," he corrected. "Actually, I usually deal with corporate law. Jasper is our top criminal attorney. I am far less flashy, but I can negotiate contracts like no one else."

Mal gasped, eyes fluttering. "Oh, my hero."

"You sound sarcastic now but just wait until you need a sponsor contract looked over. You'll mean your words then."

Mal giggled, falling against Cain's shoulder. "I'm sure I will. Anyway, about that trouble? Your friend named Roe?"

"Yes," Cain drew out the word, letting all the anger, sadness, and frustration seep out. "He is having some issues with his ex-husband. Dangerous, life-threatening issues."

"Oh, no." Mal sat up and drew his knees to his chest, wrapping his arms around them. "You can help him, right?"

"I'm trying to, but the town he lives in is not making it easy. The police there are in the ex's pocket. They've even tried to kill Roe, but everyone is claiming it was an accident. In small towns like Loriston, the sheriff and county attorney have a lot of influence." Cain pressed his lips together, trying not to reveal too much information. Mal was easy to talk to, but this was Roe's business.

"He needs to get out of there," Mal said, tone serious. "My cousin Mimi was in a bad situation with an ex-boyfriend. She was living in California at the time and didn't have any support around her. The ex was extremely charismatic and manipulative, so no one believed her when she tried to report him for harassment and stalking. Instead, their friends made excuses for his behavior and law enforcement wouldn't even make a report. It got bad enough that she couldn't take it anymore. We went to her, helped her pack and escorted her back to Thorn Creek. He even tried to follow, but my eldest brother is…well, he's just a bit scary looking. It didn't take much to send the man running."

Mal sighed. "It's not fair that she had to leave a place she enjoyed, but safety comes first. With your friend, if the worst happens and Roe is injured, he needs people who will believe him and take him seriously. Otherwise, it may go from injuries to death."

"Another cousin, huh?" Cain nudged him with his shoulder. "If she needs representation, my family know a lot of excellent lawyers all over the country. She should be able to do whatever she likes without living in fear."

Mal smiled softly, blue eyes deepening almost to black. "You are a really nice person, Cain Benson. Not just because of the offer to help Mimi. I heard all about how you and your family swept in to rescue one of the Wilsons when your brother was dating Elijah. Heros come in all shapes and sizes, you know. A person whose first instinct is to help someone else is definitely a hero. You're just as admirable as Jasper. Maybe I'll have to crush on you."

Cain's cheeks heated and he cleared his throat. "I would not be opposed to that."

Mal's eyes widened in surprise. "What now? Are you saying I might be admirable enough to interest you?"

Cain struggled to find the right words. "There's no competition, Mal. You're a completely different entity."

Mal's plump lips widened into a smile, and he leaned forward. Cain watched him move in slow motion as he pressed his mouth to Cain's in a sweet kiss.

Blood rushed to his head, and all he could hear was his own heart beating in double time. Mal tasted like coffee and Heaven. That was the only way Cain could think to describe it. Of course, he wasn't thinking much at all.

His eyes closed as heat rushed through him and pulled the omega onto his lap. His fingers tangled with Mal's silky soft hair, holding his head in place as he deepened the kiss, delving into him, soaking up every heated sensation he could. He wanted to stay exactly like that for eternity.

The heat intensified when Mal groaned and pressed as close as he could, wrapping his arms around Cain's neck and grinding his ass against Cain's dick.

Cain moaned and cradled the omega's plump bottom,

squeezing and pulling him down while he arched up. "Heavens, you feel good."

Mal moved gracefully, as if he were dancing. He writhed and arched his body, pressing against Cain. They ground together, tongues tangling and bodies moving together as if they were already one being.

In seconds, Cain was there, pleasure peaking as he came hard, Mal's body pressed tightly against him.

Mal clutched Cain's head and moaned in pleasure, curving his body around him. Cain pressed his hand against Mal's dick and traced him through the cloth. He increased the friction between them until he felt his omega's body shudder as he came.

They lingered there together, breathing hard as their kisses softened, turning sweet. "That was unexpected," Cain finally managed to say.

"A little," Mal said, pressing their foreheads together. "I've been thinking about kissing you all week. Damn it, Cain Benson. Why do you have to be so addicting?"

"No one's ever said that about me before. Boring? Several times. A workaholic? More times than I can count. Oblivious, frustrating, and cold? Yes. Addicting? Not at all." Cain grinned. "I like it. That means you need me, doesn't it? I like the idea of you needing me."

"Your admirable omegas are idiots." Mal hugged him tightly. "You made us come in our pants like fucking teenagers. This is embarrassing, but also completely glorious."

"I made us? You participated."

"Only because you're irresistible with your arched brows and too serious lips. Whose lips are too serious? Is that even a thing? I mean, obviously it is because that's how you got me."

"Trapped you, did I?" Cain laughed. "I guess I have to take responsibility for my actions."

"Yes, you do," Mal answered primly. "Come by tomorrow and I'll cook for you again."

"Yes, sir."

CHAPTER 5

The next night, Mal handed out the fake beards and googly-eyeglasses. "Noah's place has cameras, so make sure your face is covered at all times."

Cain arched a brow. "I thought this was a date."

Bianca and Van snickered.

"It is, I swear," Mal promised. "We just have a little trespassing to do first. Don't forget your beard."

Cain scowled. "Forget it. They'll recognize me anyway. At least Noah won't hound me for Bigfoot's hideout."

"Suit yourself." Mal pulled his beard in place, put the glasses on, and grabbed a hat from under the seat of his truck. "It really will be just the two of us once this is done. It's just that Van and Bianca hardly ever have the same evening off from work. I couldn't miss this opportunity."

Van patted Cain's shoulder. "You should have known better, Benson. There are a ton of omegas around that would go out with you. Picking Mal is on you."

"Hey, now." Mal should probably be offended, but Van was right.

"He's lucky to have you, Mal," Bianca pointed out, loyal as

ever. "But are you sure you should bring Truffle? Someone may recognize him."

"It's necessary." Mal patted his cat. Truffle sat happily in the pet sling Mal wore across his chest. Mal had attempted to hide his identity with a lion costume. Truffle was not amused.

"Necessary? Really?" Van snorted.

"He's feeling a bit neglected since Betty goes everywhere with us now." Mal sniffed. "Take note, Bianca. It's important that all your children feel special."

She nodded solemnly. "A child's emotional health and psychological growth are important. Noted."

Mal grabbed one of the large, stuffed horses from the back of his truck. "Here, this one is for you, Cain. It's the biggest and most special."

"I feel so important," the alpha replied, taking the horse.

Mal passed out more horses, taking two for himself. "Now remember, follow me exactly. I know where the camera placement is. I think we can miss most of them."

Van adjusted the beard on her face. "How did you figure that out?"

"I have an inside source." Mal smirked behind his beard.

"Of course you do." Cain rolled his eyes.

"Do my contacts impress you, Cain?"

"Do you want them to?"

Van wrapped an arm around Bianca and drew her closer. "Take note of way one male looks for approval from the other male. In this outlandish mating dance, one will do almost anything to garner attention."

"There's a bird in Costa Rica, the Red-capped Manakin, that moonwalks to impress potential mates." Bianca shook her head. "At least this isn't that bad."

"Oh, that's a good idea." Mal looked around. "No cameras here. Okay." He stopped in front of Cain. Bracing one foot behind him, he began a slow, awkward slide on the gravel driveway of the horse ranch, moonwalking in circles around Cain. "Imagine there's music, Cain. Are you excited? Do you want me?"

"I've never wanted you more," Cain answered, voice dry.

"Am I as good as those admirable omegas now?"

Cain barely held back a laugh as he covered his eyes. "They have nothing on you, Mal. I swear."

"Oh, look. There is a camera." Bianca pointed out.

"Oh, shit." Mal froze in place. "Let's hurry and get this done. You don't think they saw me dance, do you?"

"That's what you're worried about?" Van grumbled, opening the door to the closest barn. "Why don't they lock their doors?"

"My contact left them open for me. He's going to come lock everything down when we leave."

"I really need to know who your contact is." Cain went to the nearest empty stall and set the large stuffed horse down. "Is here alright?"

"Have its head sticking out over the gate." Bianca adjusted the horse and added her own beside it. "Like this."

Mal's heart melted as he watched his two favorite people work together. For all the mess that was Mal, Cain always handled it well. The two filled up the stall with stuffed horses, arranging them into a little horse family.

This is not good, Mal thought, heart beating fast. *Really not good.* He didn't have the luxury of falling for someone so close to the Wilson family. He sighed and placed his own horses a few stalls down, right across from Noah's miniature horses. *Not that my heart ever listens to me.*

His eyes narrowed as he surveyed their work. "Van, is that a unicorn?"

His friend shrugged and set up her own stall with a family

of unicorns. "The store only had so many stuffed horses, Mal. Give me a break."

"Noah doesn't keep unicorns. Respect the historical accuracy."

"Hold on." Bianca ran back to the truck, expertly dodging cameras, and grabbed more animals before returning. "Here's a goat, Mal. They have an actual goat somewhere around here."

"See, Van? Why can't you be more like our daughter?"

Van ignored him and placed a toy fairy on the unicorn's back. "Mind your own stall, asshole."

Cain rubbed Mal's shoulders, and his body practically liquefied. He arched up into the alpha's hands, goosebumps breaking out over his arms. "Yeah, okay. Whatever. Never stop touching me, Cain."

"Nice Mal-wrangling there, Benson." Van grinned. "You're welcome to come on these excursions any time."

"It's a tough job, but someone has to do it." Cain pulled Mal into his arms. "What are you making me for dinner?"

"Anything you want." Mal sighed happily, eyes scanning their work. Five stalls were full of stuffed horses. The real horses watched them, curious at all the commotion. "Noah will be so surprised when he comes in tomorrow. This was a good idea, Bia. You're my favorite person in the whole world."

Bianca joined their hug. "You're my favorite person too, Mal."

"Hello." Van scowled behind her fake beard. "Your mother is right here."

"We said what we meant." Mal leaned back against Cain and hugged Bianca tighter.

Twenty minutes later, they had emptied the back of Mal's truck and headed home. He dropped Van and Bianca off at their house, then parked next to his RV.

"Can I make you my favorite dish?" He fluttered his eyes and tried his best to look sweet. It was hard. What he really wanted was this man in his bed, but it was too soon for that. Mal didn't want a hook up. He wanted something more with Cain. For the first time in a long time, he was ready to take a chance. Did it make sense? No. But that didn't stop the wanting.

Cain smiled one of his serious smiles. "I would like that."

"You don't even know what it is," Mal teased as he left the truck, making sure to lock it behind them.

"God help me, but I will have to trust you." Cain looked amazed. "What have you done to me?"

"Don't blame me." Mal opened the door to the RV and grabbed the piglet trying to slip out. "Betty, my darling girl, how many messes did you leave behind today?"

Cain snorted. "Where's her harness? I'll take her for a walk to burn some of that energy."

Mal melted again. *Cain will make such a good father*, he thought, then wanted to smack himself. "Oh, yes, please and thank you. I'll get started on dinner."

Mal was surprised to find no messes, so he grabbed the ingredients he needed and went to work. Creamy mushroom and lemon spaghetti had been one of his favorites since he was a kid. It was also when of the first dishes his dad had taught him to make. The alpha loved cooking as much as Mal did, and they had spent many hours together in the kitchen.

"Truffle, don't tell anyone, but I'm going to use store bought mushrooms."

His cat gave him a look of disdain before stalking back to the bedroom. Mal knew what would happen. The cat would sit on Mal's pillow and proceed to lick his butt.

"I really shouldn't have made him wear that costume," he muttered as he took out a lemon and his zester.

Mal was dishing up the plates by the time Cain and Betty came back.

Cain took his coat off and hurriedly dried the piglet. "It started to rain."

Mal scowled out the window. "It was so nice and warm two weeks ago. Now, it's chilly and wet again."

"Betty didn't mind. Remind me to add a mudroom to my house needs list."

The piglet looked thoroughly happy as Cain rubbed her down.

"Your coat is a mess now. I have towels, you know."

Cain shrugged and sat down at the small table. "What is this? It looks really good."

"My dad's specialty," Mal said proudly. "We would spend hours foraging for mushrooms on the weekends."

"So, he's the reason you're a mycophile?"

"Yep."

"He taught me everything I know."

Cain moaned as he took the first bite. "This is really good."

They ate quietly as the rain poured, beating a loud tempo against the aluminum roof of the RV. It was cozy and warm, making Mal want to wiggle in happiness. A good meal, good company, and rain falling on a metal room? *Perfect.*

"Are you close to your father?" Cain asked, breaking the silence.

"Yes. He taught me how to cook and helped me decide what dishes to present on my show when I first started. I think he's prouder of my show than he was when I graduated from college. Of course, he never thought college was a good fit for me."

"Was he right?"

"I have a bachelor's degree in game development, but I'm making a living from a cooking show." Mal shrugged. "He was probably right, but I'm still happy I went. What are you going to do when you move to Hobson Hills?"

"I have no idea." Cain shook his head. "My brothers found their place here, and Dad and Mom are mostly happy with retirement."

"I think your dad gets bored sometimes."

"I think so too." Cain smiled softly. "You should have seen him in action when he worked at the firm. He was a civil rights attorney and took on some big cases."

"No wonder he gets bored sometimes." Mal snorted. "Maybe you and he can start a firm here in Hobson Hills. You wouldn't make money, but at least you would still help people."

"I am very lucky that money isn't an issue," Cain agreed. "My brothers and I each have a trust fund, even though Carter refuses to use his. He says he's saving it for the kids, and I can't fault him for that. I'll use most of mine for my future family too."

"I think that's a good idea, just remember that you are still young and will be bored out of your mind if you don't have something to do when you move here."

"Dad is going to take me fishing."

"You can only fish for so many hours in the day." Mal paused. "Wait, I can take you foraging too. Okay, you should forget about opening a law office with your dad and become my assistant."

Cain gave him a considering look. "What kind of perks are there?"

"Good meals and free kisses."

"I'm in."

Mal grinned. "I didn't say who the kisses would come from."

Cain eyed the pet bed where Betty and Truffle slept. "I

should know better than to jump into an ambiguous contract."

Mal chuckled, a lightness spreading through him. Cain wanted *him*. "Don't worry. I'll give you kisses too."

Cain leaned forward, face solemn. "Are you alright with this." He waved a hand between them. "With us? I don't do things half-way Mal."

"Are you alright with this?" Mal asked instead of answering. "Until last night, I wasn't sure that you were even attracted to me. You're in love with Jasper."

"I'm *not* in love with Jasper. I thought I could possibly fall in love with him." Cain scowled. "There's a difference."

"Do you not think so anymore?" Mal tilted his head, curious about Cain's use of past tense. Trust a lawyer to pick and choose his words carefully.

Cain's lips curved upward, his eyes shining with humor. "I think my tastes have drastically changed over the course of a week. I'm more interested in eccentric omegas now. One who is still admirable but is also completely unique."

Mal grinned and pointed to his chest. "I've been called eccentric. Okay, maybe I've been called weird, but same thing, right?"

Cain nodded. "They are basically synonyms of one another."

"I'm sure someone out there admires me," Mal continued. "My confidential informant really likes all the pranks I pull on the Wilsons. He's nice enough that he will say he admires me if I ask him to."

"I think more people admire you than you realize." Cain took his hand. "Are you alright with this?" he asked again. "You said you were ready to move on, but this is fast."

Mal couldn't help but laugh. "My family's motto is basically 'fall fast and love completely.'"

"Now you really have to explain that." Cain laughed. "Are

you secretly a Wilson? That seems to be their family motto too."

Mal winced and promptly ignored Cain's question. "Let me tell you a story. It all began with my paternal grandparents, David Reed and Vivian Marks."

"Should we get comfortable? Is this a long story?" Cain smiled, brown eyes sparkling.

"Absolutely." Mal stood and sat on the sofa. He patted the cushion beside him. "Come along."

Cain sat down and pulled Mal into his arms, adjusting them until they were comfortable.

Mal soaked up the warmth of the man's embrace, savoring the smell of Cain and rain. "Grandpa was born out of wedlock in a time when society was not very accepting of things like that. His mom had a one-night stand with an omega that lived a few towns over. Her parents were horrified, especially when they found out the omega had already met and married an alpha. They refused to let their daughter ruin a proper relationship, so they convinced her to not even tell the omega she was pregnant."

"That is not the warm and fuzzy story I thought was coming." Cain kissed Mal's cheek. "I'm sorry that happened."

"Me too." Mal sighed. "Shortly after he was born, Grandpa's mom died. His grandparents raised him, and they never let him forget that he was evidence of his mom's *sin*. Their words, not mine. It had a profound effect on Grandpa. He felt he had to act a certain way to keep his grandparents' love, so he set out to be the perfect beta man."

"What about his father? Did he ever reach out to him? Surely, he would be happier with him than with grandparents like that."

Mal shook his head. "Nope. His dad had a husband and kids of his own. His grandparents didn't want him messing that up, and he agreed with them."

"That's unfortunate."

"It really is." Mal sighed. "Grandpa would have been a lot happier growing up if he had went to his father. But he didn't. He dated the girls his grandparents introduced him to and ignored the fact that he was only attracted to other boys."

"No," Cain groaned. "That never works."

"It really doesn't." Mal snorted a laugh. "Lucky for him he met a girl named Vivian that was in the situation. She only liked girls, but her parents would never accept that. They agreed to date and eventually married. Their families were overjoyed, but they were just happy to have each other as best friends who understood and cared for one another."

"I'm happy for them?" Cain paused a moment. "I think."

"They struggled on, pretending to be the perfect heterosexual couple," Mal continued. "Somehow, they even managed to have two kids. I don't like to think of it, but some of my cousins speculated on the use of a turkey baster until Aunt Wanda heard them and threatened to tell their parents what they were talking about. That isn't important though. What's important is that they finally couldn't take their overbearing families anymore and moved across the country to Thorn Creek, Washington."

"Good for them." Cain hugged him. "They didn't have a conventional love, but it's still beautiful. I like this story."

"Oh, I'm not done yet." Mal settled his head on Cain's shoulder. "A few years down the road, my dad was about six, I think, Grandma Vivi worked at a local newspaper. She had a set routine. She would have breakfast with Grandpa and the kids, go to work, eat lunch at a diner nearby, go back to work, then head home. One day, that all changed."

Mal let the silence permeate.

He waited and waited.

"The suspense," Cain finally complained. "Why are you like this?"

"I enjoy the pain of others." Mal shrugged. "Anyway, one day, a new waitress started at the diner. She was a single mother of three, newly divorced and struggling to find what was missing in her life. Guess what was missing?"

"Hmm." Cain's voice rumbled through Mal. "A Grandma Vivi-shaped something?"

"Yes." Mal practically crowed. "They met and fell in love at first sight. First freakin' sight, Cain! Grandpa was beyond happy for them and fully supported the relationship. Adelaide's ex-husband was slower to come around, but he's a decent man, so eventually, with Grandpa's help, he came to terms with things. He traveled a lot for work, that's why their marriage failed, but he loved his family. He's Uncle Ron to everyone now. Grandma Vivi, Grandma Addy, and Uncle Ron."

"Okay." Cain sounded impressed. "Now, that is a beautiful story. I can see why your family isn't afraid of jumping into relationships. This bodes well for me, so I fully support the family motto."

"The story isn't done, silly." Mal patted Cain's cheek. "A couple of years later, Grandpa took the kids camping. All five of them, because where one kid went, all the others had to go. Uncle Ron learned this the hard way."

"Five? That's a lot."

"I agree." Mal nodded. "While he was there, he met a young widower – an omega that had lost his alpha a few years prior. The man had two kids of his own, both under four. Why he was out camping with them, I don't even know. But guess what?"

"Grandpa David fell in love at first sight?"

Mal laughed. "Correct. Then it was Grandpa David and

Grandpa Lucas. Five kids became seven. Then, they became eight when Grandpa Lucas got pregnant again."

"Poor Uncle Ron," Cain whispered. "He was probably struggling with only three at first. Then five. Then eight."

Mal's body shook with laughter. "Seriously. The man had to bring home presents for everyone each time he visited. He didn't hesitate, though. Took to being an uncle really well. Even for us grandkids." Mal smiled softly. "He brought me cookbooks from all over the world. They're in storage now, but I treasure them. He's retired and lives in Thorn Creek but still manages to find the best books for me for my birthday."

"No love at first sight for Uncle Ron?" Cain asked, sounding sad.

"Uncle Ron says his true love was traveling the world and having his family to come home to."

"Alright. That explains why you said your family tree was a forest instead of one tree." Cain smiled. "It really is a lovely story. What about your mom's parents? Do they have a story?"

"Grandpa Paul and Grandma Kat. They're completely normal." Mal shook his head. "Met in college, got married after a few years of dating. So very normal."

"I suppose one side of your family should be."

"Agreed." Mal leaned up and brushed a soft kiss against Cain's chin. "So, you see, I'm not afraid of a little risk. I think you're worth it."

Cain leaned down and kissed him. Mal melted into the alpha's taste, savoring every feeling bubbling inside him. The anticipation and excitement of something new. The eagerness to know everything about his alpha.

Loving Rick had never been like this. Maybe because Mal knew Rick never felt romantic toward him. It had been misery and joy all at once.

Cain pulled back, breathing heavily. "We're agreed? We will see where this goes?"

"Agreed." Mal pulled Cain down for another kiss. There was no fear or hesitation. Wherever their connection went, Mal knew he'd never be the same.

CHAPTER 6

A few weeks later, Cain forced himself to mingle with the guests at Walter Libby's birthday party. It was a prime networking event, and one he normally enjoyed. Walter was a decent sort, and many of the guests were family friends. All Cain wanted, however, was to be sitting in an RV, eating interesting food, and listening to Mal's stories about his family.

Cain had flown to Maine five weekends in a row, and it was exhausting. He had reluctantly chosen to stay in Atlanta this weekend, but he missed Mal. He had already watched all his cooking videos several times and even joined his yoga sessions. The sessions were actually helping him handle his stress and sleep better. Not that he would ever tell Mal that. The omega was smug enough as is.

"Then, the aliens arrived and ordered probes for everyone," Roe said, surprising Cain.

"What?" Cain looked down at his friend.

"You weren't listening to me." Roe tsked. "Where is that head of yours?"

"Up in the clouds," Jasper said, snickering. "He's been out of it all month."

"That's not like you." Roe eyed him. "What's going on?"

Cain sniffed. "You don't need to worry about me. Instead, let's worry about the two assholes who just walked in."

Roe and Jasper both turned to look at the door.

"The one time I decide to attend a party." Roe sighed. "Of course they're here."

James and Gabriel Dorsey both smiled angelically as they entered the ballroom. The pair made a handsome couple, but only from the outside. Inside, they were pure rot.

"Ignore them." Jasper scowled.

Cain narrowed his eyes, watching the couple move gracefully about the room, blending well with the well-dressed, wealthy guests. The two were relatively popular among the younger members of Atlanta's high society. The older members had long memories, however. They knew James had basically stolen the Dorsey family business from Roe. They had been friends with Roe's grandfathers and knew exactly what would happen if the two men were still alive.

"Who the hell invited James Dorsey?" Walter asked, walking by Cain and his friends. "He's going to spend the whole night trying to get me to invest with him again."

Jasper smiled sweetly. "That is a common theme now, Roe. James lost a lot of clients because of the way he treated you."

"That just makes him more dangerous." Cain gave Roe a serious look. "Be careful. You have unintentionally hit the pride of both of those snakes. James isn't liking the consequences of divorcing you, and Gabriel hates being constantly compared to you."

Roe rolled his eyes. "Gabriel is absolutely stunning. He'll come out on top of any comparison."

"Maybe if no one spoke to him," Jasper said, grinning. "He

is the shallowest person I've ever met and all it takes is thirty seconds of speaking to him to know it."

"Just be careful," Cain repeated. "Yes, Gabriel is shallow, but he also literally tried to hire someone to kill you."

"That was a misunderstanding." Roe waved away his concerns. "I'm going to go talk to Walter, then head home. I have kids I need to make sure are in bed."

"I half-way hope they try something." Jasper waited to speak until Roe was with Walter. "I just want an hour with them in front of a judge. That's all it will take."

Cain smiled softly and studied Jasper. A month ago, he wouldn't have been able to take his eyes off the omega. Now, Jasper was firmly entrenched in Cain's mind as a friend. It was amazing to see how spending time with a smooth-talking trickster could put things in perspective.

"You're drifting again." Jasper laughed. "Come on, man. Get it together."

"Sorry." Cain winced. "I do worry about Roe. He isn't taking the situation as seriously as he should."

"All we can do is be there when it goes bad." Jasper gave James and Gabriel a calculating look. "It will go bad. I can feel it."

"I will call our security company tomorrow," Cain said. "I want someone readily available if Roe needs protection."

"Good idea." Jasper cleared his throat. "Now, stop distracting me and explain what is going on with you."

Cain fought a smile. "I met someone."

A bright smile spread across Jasper's handsome face, then dimmed. "Please tell me it isn't one of those omegas you usually date. They're nice and all, but they do not suit you."

Cain laughed and Jasper stared at him in amazement.

"You laughed." Jasper shook his head. "What is happening?"

"He's in Hobson Hills right now, and, to answer your

question, he is not like the omegas I usually date. He is so much better."

"Hobson Hills?" Jasper asked. "Does that mean you really will be leaving us? I hoped you would change your mind."

"I'm looking at houses already." Cain bit his lip. "I haven't told my parents yet. Or my brothers. Or anyone else really."

Jasper nodded. "My lips are sealed. I'll miss you, but your happiness comes first. This man makes you smile and laugh. I like that for you. Plus, I have already made sure I can practice in Maine since your dad moved there. If you ever need me, I'll come running."

"I would like to say we won't need a criminal attorney, but knowing Mal as I do, it's good to know you can help."

Jasper snorted a laugh. "I really have to meet this man."

A few hours later, Cain finally arrived home. His apartment was clean and orderly, but oh so quiet. Cain missed Betty and Truffle, despite the mess they made. Mal's RV could easily fit into Cain's living room, but it had come to feel more like home than the place Cain had lived for years now.

He sighed and fell onto the couch, then grabbed his phone.

Mal answered the video call quickly. "Are you wearing a tux? Oh, you are. Take pictures. Now."

Cain chuckled. "Nice to see you too, weirdo."

"Weirdo is not a pet name. Try sweetheart or darling."

"You are neither sweet nor charming enough to be either."

"Why do I like you again?" Mal's blue eyes narrowed.

Cain used the phone to scan over his torso.

"Oh yeah, those shoulders. Plus, you're in a tux. Take. A. Picture."

Cain ignored him and laughed. "What did you have for dinner tonight?"

"My confidential informant brought me some fresh eggs and milk, so I made a delicious veggie quiche before I snuck into the brewery and filled Abel's desk drawers with dog toys shaped like beer bottles."

"Oh, my sweet, darling…," Cain began, grinning when Mal looked overjoyed. "… little weirdo," Cain finished. "The Wilsons must think they're cursed."

Mal scowled. "Just for that, I'm not going to make this quiche for you when you come back."

"I apologize." Cain tried for a pathetic look. "You are the kindest, sweetest darling I've ever met."

"Better." Mal smirked. "Now, take the dang pictures, Cain. You look really good in a tux."

A WEEK LATER, Cain was more than ready to murder Roe's ex and retreat to Hobson Hills so Mal could cook him something delicious. He paced the floor of the Loriston Emergency Room, hands shaking as he texted Mal. *Roe is alive. No life-threatening injuries.*

Get him out of there, Mal texted back. *It doesn't even have to be Hobson Hills, but he needs to get away from the threat.*

Cain ran his hands through his hair, then slumped down into the seat.

"The doctor said he is going to be okay," Tris, Roe's eldest son, said. He wrapped an arm around Daphne's shoulders. Roe's middle child was shaking worse than Cain's hands.

"He could have died." Daphne sobbed. "I don't want to lose Dad. He's all we have, Tris."

Cain left his chair and hugged the two. "You all are not alone. We'll keep him safe, Daphne. I promise."

"How?" she asked, rubbing her face against his shoulder.

"We get you all out of here." He hugged her tighter and called Sheriff McKenzie.

"Sheriff McKenzie speaking." The older man's rough, authoritative voice was a welcome respite. The situation wasn't one Cain could easily handle, and he was legitimately scared for Roe and the kids.

"Hello, Sheriff," he said. "This is Cain Benson. I think you know my parents and my brothers, Carter and Caden."

"Yes, I do."

"I have a favor to ask," Cain said, voice grim. "It's important."

"What can I do for you?" Mack asked, no hesitation in his voice.

Cain did his best to control his anger. Clarity was needed here. "I need a safe place for a client and his family to stay for a few months. Someone is trying to kill him."

Daphne shook harder, and Tris's eyes watered. The eldest had stayed strong all night but was almost at his limit.

Cain kissed the top of Daphne's head and stepped away, hoping the kids wouldn't hear the rest. "He's a good friend with three kids. Someone ran him off the road earlier today. His car was totaled, and he could have died. We suspect his ex-husband hired someone to do it. He's tried before. We need to get him out of this town, Sheriff. Can you help?"

"You bring them here as soon as you can. I have a big house that's right down the street from the police station. We'll keep him safe."

Cain felt the tension leave his body like water from a faucet. They really weren't alone in this. "Thank you. I will call you back with details as soon as I can."

"Good deal."

The call ended and Cain immediately video called Mal. The omega looked as worried as Cain felt.

"What's happening?"

"Sheriff McKenzie is going to watch over them. He said to bring them as soon as possible."

"Of course he did." Mal bit his lip. "Do they know who it was that ran him off the road?"

"Witnesses gave a description of the vehicle." Cain rubbed his eyes. "Jasper is pushing the police. Even if they are corrupt here, they can't blatantly ignore this. We're going to stay involved. If they don't do their job, then we will. I already scheduled a bodyguard for Roe and the kids. His name is Wally, and he is prepared to stay with them until this is over."

"Good." Mal sighed. "I'm so sorry, Cain. At least Roe is alright. Hobson Hills will be good for him."

Cain nodded. "It will. I'm just worried about him. He looked so defeated, Mal. This situation has been going on for years. It's been Hell for him."

"For you too," Mal said softly.

Cain swallowed hard. "I hate feeling helpless. I can only imagine how Roe feels."

"You aren't helpless." Mal's brow furrowed. "You and the admirable Jasper will make sure those assholes pay for this."

Cain's smile felt sharp and pointy. "Yes, we will."

CHAPTER 7

"Lower your knees to the mat, then slide onto your belly," Mal instructed, demonstrating for the camera trained on him. "Sphinx pose."

Truffle hopped onto his back, settling in and purring loudly.

They were nearing the end of the session, and Mal couldn't keep his eyes from straying to the Zoom grid screen streaming on his smart tv. Cain was in the top right corner, next to Bom, an elderly Korean woman Mal had met in Florida a couple of years ago. His live yoga sessions had grown over the years. He now held two sessions every day, and so far, Cain joined him for each one.

"One more deep breath, then let's move into child pose." Mal smoothly changed positions, Truffle adjusting to stay in place on his back. "Knees on the mat, toes touching. Widen your knees as much as possible." He checked over the other ten members. "Good, good. Now walk your hands out in front of you and fold on down."

He let his breath out and cleared his mind. "Five breaths here. Let's ground ourselves. Check-in and self-reflect."

The quiet sound of breathing and Truffle's purrs settled the chaotic mess gurgling inside him. It was a new mess, a fresh and delicious agony. It had taken years for Mal to fall completely for Rick, but damn if he wasn't on the cusp with Cain after a couple of months.

I refuse to fall in love so quickly, he told himself, breathing deeply. *I am not my grandparents. It's just an intense case of like.*

Mal moved through the rest of the short session, Truffle finally settling on the mat beside him. "Let's end in the Siddhasana pose for some box breathing. This is meant to help reduce mental clutter. Remember to use a count of four for each step. Inhale, hold the breath in, exhale, hold the breath out. All for a count of four. Four corners, like a box."

Mal counted out the beats for the first breath. "Good, now five more breaths."

The session ended with a long, drawn-out *om*, and people began to log out, looking more at peace than when they had signed in.

"Fuck me, bro, I needed that," Tripp, one of Mal's friends from college, said, looking refreshed.

"Life too hard for a stockbroker?" Bom asked, wryly.

"Nothing I can't handle, beautiful." Tripp grinned. "You going to let me make you some money today? No extra charge, just send me some of your homemade kimchi."

Mal cleared his throat, fighting a smile. "No soliciting during zoom calls."

Bom rolled her eyes. "Pretty boy knows he's not getting my money, Mal. I will send you some Kimchi though."

"You're the best, Bom." Tripp looked happy.

"Don't let him charm you out of your kimchi," Marta, a young woman Mal had met in Arizona, said, stretching her legs out in front of her. "Next thing you know, you'll have to feed him every day and get rid of his fleas. That's what happens with strays."

"Marta, my sweet, lovely Marta," Tripp blew a kiss. "Are you ready to leave that wife of yours? Shayna and I will take good care of you. We'd make a happy throuple."

Marta snorted. "I don't know how your wife puts up with you." She stretched her arms, then let out a painful yelp before cupping her breasts.

Bom looked sympathetic. "Is the baby not latching right?"

Tripp winced. "Your poor nips."

Marta grimaced. "My nipples are cracked more than Tripp's head. I love my baby girl, but I swear I don't want to feed her ever again."

"Try a warm compress and a salt-water rinse," Bom said, nodding firmly. "That will help."

"Shayna works with a lot of new moms at her clinic," Tripp said. "I'll ask her to text you. She'll fix you up with whatever you need."

"It sounds like you're dealing for your wife," Mal said, chuckling.

"Nah, nothing illegal," Tripp said, grinning again. "More like medi-honey and nipple cream."

"That is better than cocaine for a new, breastfeeding mama." Bom grinned.

"Enough about my nipples." Marta groaned. "Benson, how's your friend doing?"

Cain, looking as calm and solemn as usual, nodded to them. "His case is progressing too slowly. That's all I can really say about it."

"Of course," Bom nodded respectfully. "You must keep privileged information. I am following the case in the news too. I hope those villains get what they deserve."

"I hope so too, but it will be hard." Tripp frowned. "I know people like that. They have more money and power than they should and use it in all the wrong ways."

"Actions have consequences," Cain said, voice hard. "I will make sure they understand that."

A shiver ran down Mal's spine. "Super lawyer," he whispered, a little in awe of Cain. It had only been a few weeks since Roe was injured, but Cain and Jasper were working the case hard. Every night, Cain would call and vent with Mal. They were facing opposition at all fronts in Loriston. Mal had faith, though. Cain was persistent and smart.

The others in the group gradually logged out, eventually leaving just Cain and Mal.

"I saw Roe at the bookstore in town the other day," Mal said. "He looks okay. I think he likes Hobson Hills and the sheriff."

The corner of Cain's mouth lifted in a smirk. "He *really* likes the sheriff."

"Who wouldn't? Sheriff McKenzie is one fine man."

Cain frowned. "I feel like I should be jealous here, but it's hard to be when I agree."

Mal laughed. "You'll appreciate this then. I heard a lot of the omegas in town are messing with them. They keep flirting with the sheriff to make Roe jealous."

Cain exhaled loudly, looking torn. "I really want to see that. Damn it. I need to stay here for a little longer. Jasper oversees the case, but I'm helping as much as I can with research and searching for evidence. It's taking longer than it should to get the courts to take Roe's situation seriously."

"I'll take pictures when I see them being cute."

"You could just introduce yourself to Roe," Cain said dryly. "He would like you."

"Not happening." Mal shook his head. "I gather my intel from a distance. Trust me, it's better that way."

"Gather intel?" Cain narrowed his eyes. "Convince me that you are not a spy again."

Mal chuckled and blatantly ignored the order.

"Wait, if you only gather intel from a distance, what happened with me?" Cain asked, a slow smile spreading across his face. "I'm special, aren't I?"

"The ego on you." Mal rolled his eyes. "You're the exception strictly because you help me prank the Wilsons. That's all."

"If you say so." Cain smirked. "I regret nothing. I'm starting to really enjoy the pranks, especially the ones on Ernie. We have history."

Mal rolled his eyes. "Your brothers are allowed to have friends. You shouldn't be so jealous."

Cain shrugged. "Let me enjoy what I enjoy."

Mal cackled happily. "Okay. You *are* the best partner-in-pranks that I've ever had. I'll be more understanding."

"I'm honored," Cain said wryly.

Mal hugged Truffle close. "My confidential informant told me that Ernie is begging the town council to support a Bigfoot festival for October, next year."

Cain snorted. "Of course he is."

"When are you coming back?" Mal asked, forcing the longing from his voice. "We have more pranks to pull."

"Next weekend," Cain said, smiling. "I'll come up next weekend." His brown eyes warmed. "You promised to cook for me again."

Mal's heartbeat increased, and he swallowed the lump in his throat. "I have a bruschetta recipe I want to try."

"Sounds delicious." Cain's smile was different this time. He logged out, leaving the screen blank.

"Sexy smile," Mal whispered, body heating. "Flipping heck. Why does he have to be so perfect? I very much should *not* fall for a Benson. They're too close to the Wilsons and that would upset Grandpa David."

Mal picked Truffle up and held the large cat in front of his face. "It's okay, Mal," he spoke for Truffle from the side of his mouth. "Grandpa David doesn't have to know."

Mal hugged Truffle. "You are so smart. Thank you, Truffle. I feel better now."

He wasn't sure that he had ever felt this happy in a relationship. Mal was constantly surprised at how easy it all felt. Cain was very different from Mal, but somehow, they fit. They bickered here and there, but always in fun. Learning about one enough, emotionally and physically, was comfortable and exciting all at once.

"Fuck it, Truffle. Grandpa always likes to tell me that life is too short to waste trying to be someone else. I like me. I think Cain might like me too. I'm gonna risk it."

His cat nuzzled his head against Mal's chin.

"Love you, buddy."

The day moved slowly. Mal prepared for a new cooking episode, placed a large order online for ping pong balls to be sent to Van's house for easy pickup, and took Betty and Truffle on a long hike into the state forest near Hobson Hills. It was dark by the time they got back, and his stomach was telling him food was needed.

He parked his truck near his RV and grabbed Truffle's leash. "Are you ready for some yum yums?"

"Meowr," Truffle rumbled loudly.

Betty snuffled from the back, already asleep.

"Poor little piglet," he cooed, picking her up.

"Need help?"

Mal let out a squeal that was absolutely, completely manly. "Bianca, don't sneak up on me like that." He turned to her. "What's wrong?" he asked in a whisper, taken about to see her crying.

"Paula is so stupid." Bianca picked up Truffle, lip trembling. "I hate her."

"Come inside, sweetness. Tell me what happened." Mal

unlocked his door and carried Betty to the pet bed. "Are you hungry? How about some alfredo?"

"I love alfredo," she said, settling on the sofa with Truffle.

Mal washed his hands, then pulled out the ingredients. "I made the fettuccine last week and the heavy cream is from Farm Fresh. You know it's gonna be good."

"So modest," Bianca laughed and wiped her eyes.

"Now, start at the beginning. Why is Paula stupid?"

Bianca squeezed her eyes shut. "She's so judgmental. I'm an adult and know what I'm doing. She has no right to tell me that I'm –" She stopped mid-sentence. "Anyway, she makes me feel like *I'm* the stupid one." She shook her head and opened her eyes. "I don't have to listen to her shit. I *do* know what I'm doing."

Mal winced, unsure how to comfort her. "Well, you aren't an adult, you're only sixteen, but you do have a good head on your shoulders. I would trust you with Truffle and Betty, and that means something."

"I'm basically an adult," she said, rolling her eyes. "I have a job and paid for the Vespa."

"There's a lot more to being an adult than having a part-time job and a vehicle." Mal waved his cheese grater at her. "That's a whole other topic, though. What did Paula do?"

Bianca stared at him for a moment. "You'll tell Mom anything I say."

"Yes, I will." He nodded and vigorously grated his dwindling block of parmesan cheese.

Bianca sighed. "I am seeing someone."

"Ha!" Mal gave her a smug look. "We knew it. Who are they? What do they look like? What's their family like?"

"I'm not saying." She gave him a firm look. "You and Mom wouldn't understand. Paula doesn't. She said it's wrong, but love is never wrong."

Mal gave her a sympathetic look. Paula and her dad had

seemed nice, but a lot of bigots seemed nice before they found out you weren't straight.

"Why do you think your mom and I wouldn't understand? We aren't exactly a conservative family."

"You just won't." Bianca huffed and let Truffle leave her ever tightening embrace. "I shouldn't have told Paula."

"It's hard to lose a friend, especially over something like this." Mal set a saucepan on the stove and began to slowly cook the butter and chopped garlic. "Your mom and I will love you, no matter what. Even if for some reason we don't approve of who you're seeing. Though, seriously, I don't expect that to happen."

Bianca looked particularly stubborn as she grabbed Truffle again. "I'm not telling you who it is."

"When you're ready, I'm here." Mal added seasoning to the pot as the butter and garlic sizzled. "You're the daughter of my heart and I will never not love you."

She smiled and hugged Truffle. "Thank you, Mal."

CHAPTER 8

A few weeks later, Cain sat in his office and rewatched Mal's latest cooking show for the seventh time. He liked the longer formats better, so he watched the full videos from Mal's website instead of the shorter ones posted to social media.

When cooking, simple doesn't always mean easy, Mal said on the screen. *It takes more time, which not everyone can afford to give. Be kind to yourself and don't feel guilty if you have to cheat a bit.* He wore a plain, black t-shirt and a bright, floral-patterned chef headwrap. To Cain, he was the most beautiful person in the world, and Cain wanted to be there with him.

"Mr. Benson? Your three o'clock is here." Lyle, Cain's personal assistant, gave him a tentative look from the door. "Do you want me to reschedule?"

He sighed and put his phone away. "No, Lyle. Send him in."

Frank Long came in shortly after, his large, muscular frame filling the doorway.

Cain stood up and held his hand out. "Thank you for coming, Mr. Long."

The older alpha shook his hand and settled his bulk carefully into a chair. "As many years as we've known each other, you can call me Frank."

Cain nodded solemnly. They did this every time they met, but the man was a professional colleague, so Cain could not force himself to be informal. His family had used Frank's private investigative security firm since before Cain was born.

Frank sighed. "Of course, you won't." He placed a thick file on the desk. "Okay, Benson. I'll get to the point. We've kept surveillance on the Dorsey couple 24/7. They both have met with known contract criminals. The list is in my report. Green highlights are non-violent and not considered dangerous, yellow have no violent charges or convictions against them but *are* reportedly violent, red have killed before."

Cain nodded and made a note to contact the green highlighted names. They might be willing to share what James and Gabriel discussed.

"The deep dives we did on the new employees James hired were interesting too. One was hired as a personal aide, but he's a private detective. Guess what he's been doing?"

"I imagine he is searching for Roe."

Frank grinned. "Correct. He has also been looking closely at you and Jasper."

Cain scowled.

"I advise no more trips to Hobson Hills until this is over."

Cain fought the urge to throw the file in front of him across the room. Frustration threatened to bubble over each day that he was away from Mal. *Think of Roe and the kids*, he reminded himself, closing his eyes and taking a deep breath. *They need me here.*

Over the weeks since Roe's accident, Cain had worked hard. He'd easily established motive. When James divorced Roe and took full control of the Dorsey investment firm, several clients had severed ties with him. Each of those clients was willing to testify and describe how desperate James had been to win them back and how angry he was when it didn't work.

As for Gabriel, Cain had several witnesses willing to testify about how Gabriel was constantly compared to Roe at business functions. Roe may think that he wasn't as well-liked as Gabriel in their social circles, but he underestimated how shallow society was. Gabriel was handsome and charming, but he wasn't Roe. He wasn't born a Dorsey. One of Gabriel's maids even told him about how obsessed Gabriel was with surpassing Roe and how violently angry he would get when nothing worked.

Motive, they had. Facts were what they needed. "What about connections to the Loriston police?" he asked.

Frank nodded. "We discovered several connections. The officials of Loriston are invited to every party James and Gabriel throw. James even helped the sheriff join his golf club. More importantly, we have evidence that each time Roe went to the police, James made a large donation to the police force. That is damning enough, but after some digging, we found out Gabriel used to date the mayor of Loriston. Reportedly, the man is still in love with him. If you can legally get hands on communication between the mayor and the sheriff, you will see that the mayor pressured the sheriff to treat James and Gabriel like royalty."

"You have already seen those conversations," Cain said rather than asked. Frank legally obtained all information he gave his clients. He had to for it to stand up in court. However, that didn't mean he never came across the stray nugget of information through questionable means.

"I can neither confirm nor deny that." Frank smiled. "Get a warrant and they might find many dirty dealings between the mayor, sheriff, and the Dorsey couple."

"We can bring this to the state Attorney General. Thank you, Mr. Long." Cain had already tried working with the county attorney, but suspected they were as corrupt as the sheriff and mayor since they had completely ignored all communication from him.

Frank leaned forward, smirking. "Before I go, I wanted to ask you about the house you're buying. Do you really need all that space?"

Cain narrowed his eyes. "Nosy."

"I didn't tell anyone." Frank held his hands up. "I didn't even deep dive you. Wally did. I just found out from him."

Cain picked up his phone, cheeks heating. "It's a four-bedroom lake cabin on ten acres. There is a large garden area and plenty of pasture for a Kunekune. Look at the kitchen."

Frank stared at him for a moment, clearly shocked. "You never talk to me about anything personal."

Cain sniffed. "Just look at the kitchen."

Frank gave him a suspicious look then stared at the picture on his phone. "Do you even cook? Why would you need that big of a kitchen?"

Cain ignored him. "The breakfast nook looks out over the lake, and the other windows look out over the garden. It is quite peaceful. Oh, and those are granite countertops. You can put hot things right on them. They're easy to keep clean too."

"So, you *are* moving to Hobson Hills and apparently you're going to take up cooking." Frank eyed him. "What's a Kunekune?"

"A small breed of pig." He scrolled through his phone and showed Frank another picture. "This is the sunroom. It will be perfect for yoga."

"You do yoga?"

"It helps improve strength and mobility." Cain frowned. "I

really should refrain from traveling until this is over, shouldn't I?"

Frank gave him a sympathetic look. "James and Gabriel know you are friends with Roe Dorsey. You could lead them right to him."

Cain set his phone down. "Noted. Thank you again, Mr. Long."

"Aww, we're back to formal Cain again?"

"Does formal Cain ever really go away?" Jasper asked, leaning against the door frame.

Cain shuffled some of the papers on his desk. "I do have work to finish. Have Lyle write you a check on the way out."

Frank ignored him, looking back over his shoulder. "He was showing me pictures of the house."

Jasper laughed and came inside, sitting in the empty chair next to Frank. "He loves that house, but it doesn't suit him at all. It's nothing like his apartment."

Cain flushed. "It suits Mal and I perfectly."

"Mal?" Frank pinned him with his gaze. "Now, this is getting good. Who is Mal?"

"His boyfriend," Jasper answered, propping his chin on a fist. "Is it that serious, though? You just started dating, but you're buying a house for the two of you. That's a huge step."

Cain cleared his throat, face heating again. "I am joining his D&D group tonight. It is *very* serious."

Jasper and Frank slowly turned to look at one another before laughing uncontrollably. "That's how you judge how serious your relationship is?" Frank snorted.

"Campaigns can last for months or even years." Cain gave them both a disdainful look. "Obviously this means Mal plans on me being around for that long."

Jasper gave him a gentle look. "I'm sure he does. Nothing says love like D&D."

Frank started laughing again. "What's your character like?"

"I am an orc warrior, but Mal said not to get too attached to my first character. The DM likes to haze newcomers, so he will likely give my character a terrible, uncurable curse or kill me. I will probably have to start again."

Frank shook his head. "I'm sorry but I need to go now. I have to call your father to talk, uh, business. Yeah, business."

Frank stood and practically skipped to the door, grinning back at Cain as he left the room.

"I thought you wanted to keep moving to Hobson Hills and Mal a secret for a little longer," Jasper said, wincing. "You shouldn't have said anything to him."

"He wanted to see pictures of the house."

"Did *he* want to see them, or did *you* want to show them to him?" Jasper asked, laughing.

Cain shrugged. "Anyway, Frank's report is thorough, and I plan to start interviewing some of the contract criminals James and Gabriel have spoken with after I contact the Attorney General."

"I'll help." Jasper smiled. "Let's get this done so Roe is safe and you can focus on D&D."

LATER THAT NIGHT, Cain sat at his kitchen bar and arranged his laptop and D&D rulebook. He was nervous. Like he had told Jasper, this was a big deal for Mal. Rick, the dungeon master, was the old friend that Mal used to love. The man he still cared for. Cain didn't like it. Many of his past partners had described Cain as cold and uncaring. From the way Mal described his friend, Rick was funny and kind. Not at all cold and uncaring. What if seeing them interact made Mal realize that Cain wasn't as good of a catch as he thought?

His phone beeped and he picked it up, smiling when Mal's face appeared on the screen. His omega looked cute, his brown hair a mess of curls and his freckles there for all to see. He wore pointy ear tips as well since his character was an elf.

"Are you ready for this?" Mal asked, grinning.

"I have the rulebook and your personalized guide with me." Cain set his phone on the stand next to his laptop. "Are you sure they won't mind me joining?"

"I'm sure." Mal blew him a kiss. "We're in a tavern, recruiting mercenaries for help with our next adventure. It's the perfect place to bring in a new character. Are you ready?"

"I have my second character sheet filled out just in case."

Mal winced. "Sorry about the extra work. Rick always hazes the newbies. When Tripp first joined us after he began dating Shayna, Rick cursed him with rotting limbs. Every time he attacked something, a limb would fall off. Tripp couldn't stand it, so he rushed a monster with a higher challenge rating and died. Rick made us all go back and start again so Tripp could create a new character."

"I didn't know Tripp played." Cain tilted his head as he thought of the loud man that joined Mal's yoga sessions. He really didn't seem the type to have the patience and imagination.

"Oh, he doesn't." Mal chuckled. "He hates it and calls us dorks. He just played at the beginning because he was trying to impress Shayna."

"That sounds like him." Cain studied Mal's face, soaking up his semi-presence like a flower in the sun. "What did you do today?"

"I worked on my next cooking episode. I decided to do an episode on drying herbs. Then Bianca and I went foraging with Truffle and Betty. I found some wild blueberries and strawberries. Bianca found some raspberry and blackberry bushes, but they're not ready to pick yet. We'll go back in a few weeks."

"How is Bianca doing?" Cain asked. Mal had told him about the fight with Paula.

"She's out of school for the summer and working a lot at the grocery store. When she isn't there, usually she's with me. Her and Paula haven't made up yet, but I think they will. Even if I don't know who Bianca is dating, I can't understand why Paula is being so close-minded about it." Mal shook his head. "Enough about me. How are you doing with Roe's case?"

Cain was quiet for a moment.

"You don't have to tell me anything," Mal said, voice soft.

"No, I want to." Cain sighed. "James Dorsey tried to hire someone to assault me and Jasper in the hopes that he could intimidate us into dropping the case."

"What?" Mal's eyes narrowed, filling with rage. He looked like a very angry wood elf which made Cain smile.

"Earlier today, we interviewed some shady people the couple has been talking to and one of them admitted what he was asked to do. Good news is the man turned Dorsey down, but will testify. Bad news is, we don't know if Dorsey was successful in hiring someone else to do the job."

"That son of a –"

The computer beeped as others started signing into the roleplaying platform Mal and his friends used. The game tabletop appeared and four other faces popped up in tiny boxes at the top of the screen.

Mal growled. "We'll continue this conversation later."

Cain nodded, smiling despite the stress of the day. His angry wood elf was a healing balm. "Don't worry. We both have guards now. The firm insisted."

"They better have."

Mal ended the call, then signed into the gaming platform. Mal's group consisted of two other men and one woman.

One of the men, a handsome blond, smiled wide. "Hey there, Cain. I'm Rick. It's really nice to meet you. Mal has never invited anyone to our game before. You have to be special."

"Shut up, Rick." Mal's cheeks flushed as he cleared his throat. "Anyway, this is Shayna, Rick, and Rodney. Everyone, this is my, um, boyfriend?"

"Is that a question?" Shayna asked, brown eyes twinkling with laughter. "Do we get to decide?"

"I am his partner," Cain replied calmly.

"Partner in lurve." Rodney grinned.

"Exactly," Cain agreed.

Everyone except Mal laughed for a minute, then Rick took charge. "Okay, that's enough teasing. Did everyone review Cain's character sheet? He's an orc warrior specializing in axes."

"Exactly what we need." Shayna clapped. "We have a druid, a thief, and a priest, but we really need a tank."

Rick sighed. "Only because our druid refuses to use any of his powerful summoned beasts."

"They may get hurt," Mal said, frowning. "My babies are special."

"You tamed the wyvern we fought last time." Rick shook a finger at the screen. "He would make a great tank."

"No." Mal shook his head. "Jojo is still healing from the damage you monsters did to him."

Shayna snorted a laugh. "Okay, so Cain, your man tries to tame every animal-like monster we come across. Sometimes he's successful, but most of the time, he's completely useless in a fight."

Cain fought a laugh. "That tracks with his personality."

"It really does."

"Hey," Mal said, scowling. "At least I don't try to seduce every humanoid monster like Rodney does. He doesn't even keep the ones he succeeds with."

Rodney shrugged. "I'm the love them and leave them type. I pick their pockets before I leave. That's something, right? Remember how we got that relic a few adventures ago?"

"I take good care of my babies." Mal sniffed.

Rick sighed. "You all give me a headache. Don't let Shayna fool you either, Cain. She's just as bad as those two. She's a priestess of Godiva, goddess of chocolate. Somehow all of her spells revolve around chocolate."

"Hail Godiva," Shayna said, and took a bite of a candy bar.

"She also focuses more on trying to do damage than heal her team. Which is her job. To heal. Did you hear that, Shayna?" Rick looked tired. "I don't know why I still play with them."

"Oh, you love us." Rodney waved away Rick's concerns. "Come on. Let's get started."

The game started as Rick went from teasing friend to deep voiced narrator. He described the forest path they walked as they journeyed toward the bandits they had chosen to pursue. Ancient trees and thick brush made the path hard to traverse. They had to go single file with Cain, their warrior in the front.

"A mysterious crate blocks your path," Rick said. "Is it treasure? A long forgotten relic from the ancients? There is only one way to know. Sourpuss, the mighty orc warrior, must open the crate."

Mal grumbled. "Of course, he does. You're going to curse him."

"No one knows what is in the crate," Rick said. "There doesn't appear to be any spell or curse cast upon it, but only Sourpuss can open the heavy lid."

Cain shrugged and rolled to open the crate.

"Sourpuss opens the crate and a cloud of mysterious dust flies around his head, soaking into his mighty pores before eventually dispersing."

"Fuck, you're probably cursed, man." Rodney winced. "Want me to find a sorcerer to seduce into helping you?"

"The orc warrior is indeed cursed," Rick said solemnly. "His large, burly frame twists and shrinks into a new form. A form of fuzzy cuteness. Sourpuss has found himself with the unbreakable curse of feline transfiguration. He has become a common housecat."

"There is nothing common about a housecat," Mal said, rolling his eyes. "Damn it, Rick."

"He can't tank as a housecat," Shayna added, sighing. "He'll have to start a new character. Why are you like this, Rick? Why?"

Cain thought in silence for a moment, ignoring the bickering of the others. "What do I look like?" he asked.

"Okay." Rick sounded surprised and looked down at his notes. "The mighty orc has become a long haired, black and white cat with green eyes."

"Okay, I can work with that." Cain nodded. "Let's continue on our journey."

Rick looked absolutely delighted. "Oh, I like him, Mal. I like him a lot."

Mal laughed. "I like him a lot too."

The adventurers continued along the path, fighting off the bandits, or, in Cain's case, weaving through their legs to trip the monsters before jumping for their throats. At one point, Rodney even tossed Cain at a boss, leading the warrior to shred the bandit leader's face.

Cain took a drink of water and fought a smile. It was the best date of his life.

"There should be a little white splotch on his left, front paw." Mal pointed at the drawing so Harper Wilson could make another note. "Otherwise, the coloring is accurate. Oh, he's going to be so cute."

Harper smiled at him, the small gap between his front teeth a testament to his Wilson ancestry. Grammy Wilson had graced all her blood related children and grandchildren with a Lauren Huttonisque smile.

"I'll have the carving for you by the end of the week, Mr. Reed. The armor will be the hardest part, so I'll send you pictures as I progress."

"Thank you."

"Of course, sir."

Mal's own smile faltered. It felt wrong to have a man only a few years younger than him call him sir and mister. He left Harper's house quickly, hoping not to run into another Wilson. He usually stuck close to the don't-talk-to-a-Wilson rule, but Harper was the best woodworker Mal knew about.

He chuckled as he thought about the night before. Cain had fit into Mal's D&D group perfectly. He'd embraced being a cat which surprised everyone. What was more surprising was that Rick had already planned a whole set of adventures on the hope that Cain would accept his curse gracefully. The thought his friend put into pranking a newb was astounding.

As he drove through town, the signs of summer were everywhere. Colorful flowers decorated the walkways, a lemonade stand perched next to the bookstore, and an ice cream truck provided a high amount of sugar to several children. Hobson Hills was really a great town. There were negatives, of course. All towns had them, especially small towns. However, there were many good people here, and, in his experience, good people made a good town.

If he were ever to settle down somewhere besides Thorn Creek, it would be here. "That would make Grandpa David so mad," he said aloud, chuckling. "Serves him right for getting me socks for Christmas when I was five."

"Sometimes I wonder about your sanity," Van said, shaking her head. She sat in the passenger seat of his truck, dressed for a day of fishing. "You know we forgot the cooler, right?"

"Crappity crap." He made a right turn. "I want my wine."

"Yes, who can fish without their merlot?" Van rolled her eyes.

"You get your beer; I get my wine." He shrugged. "No judgement."

"Who would I be if I couldn't judge?" Van looked sad.

He laughed. "I love you."

"Love you, too."

All laughter stopped when they both spotted Bianca at the door to his RV. The teenager was crying, eyes swollen, arms wrapped around herself.

"What's wrong?" Van asked, out of the truck before it had even stopped.

"Mom," she said, voice breaking.

Van wrapped her arms around her daughter and pulled her close.

Mal quickly parked the truck and ran to them. "Come inside. I'll make some hot cocoa."

Van and Bianca settled onto the couch while Mal let Betty out into the small, fenced space he had made for her next to his RV. The fencing was removable and made a nice temporary space for Betty to use the bathroom or get some sunshine.

Once the pig was settled, he went back inside and started making the cocoa. While he did, Bianca spoke through her sobs.

"He broke up with me," she squeaked. "He said I was just a slut that was trying to break up his family."

"Family?" Mal asked, his own voice rising. The stirring spoon dropped from his hand. "What does that mean? Do his parents not approve of you or something?"

"How old is this person?" Van asked, face turning red.

Bianca cried harder. "Mom, his age doesn't matter. It's just a number. I'm not telling you all who he is. He has a wife and kids. They don't need you two making a scene. I don't want to break up his family. I really don't. I just want to be with him."

"Bianca Lorraine Bell, you are sixteen years old. The age of this married man matters a great deal." Van stood up and began pacing. "He has to be over eighteen, so his ass should be in jail."

Mal went to his room and pulled Bianca's favorite blanket out of the drawer beneath the bed. "Bianca, you're not in trouble. We love you and always will." His fingers shook as he wrapped it around her, bundling her up like a burrito before hugging her. Her own shaking calmed.

Van stopped pacing and squeezed onto the couch with them, hugging Bianca from the other side. "It will be alright, sweetheart. You're not alone. We're here. We love you."

They stayed like that for a while, letting Bianca cry as long as she needed to. As her tears slowed, Mal wiggled out from their hug and went back to making hot cocoa. While he was at it, he made her favorite chocolate chip cookies too.

She took the plate of cookies and mug of cocoa from him. In seconds she had devoured two of the cookies and half the cocoa. "Maybe he was right," she finally said. "Maybe I do mess things up."

Van snorted. "I very much doubt that. Sweetheart, what happened? When did this start?"

"Last Christmas," she whispered. "Right after Jen left. Mom, he's the sweetest guy. He makes me feel special and beautiful. His age really doesn't matter. He said he was going to leave his wife. She's really not good for him and the kids. He said we'd get married and have kids of our own."

"You're too young to reasonably make those kinds of decisions," Van said, voice soft and gentle. "This man knows that. Some people will say anything to get a person to sleep with them. I don't have to know the man's name to know that he saw an innocent, beautiful girl and chose to manipulate her to get what he wanted."

"I'm not stupid." She glared at them from the covers.

"No, you're not," Mal agreed, sitting on the floor in front of them. "You're young. You've never dated anyone before. Your best friend just moved away, and you were lonely. There is nothing wrong with any of that. What's wrong is that this man saw all that and used it against you."

"He wouldn't do that."

"Why did he break up with you?" Van asked, switching gears.

Bianca began crying again. "I told him I was pregnant. He said I was a... a lying slut." She sobbed against Mal's shoulder. "I'm not lying and I'm not a sl…slut. He's the only person I've ever been with. I thought he wanted a baby."

"You're pregnant?" Van's eye twitched and Mal shook his head, silently telling her to stay cool.

"This man broke up with you because you're pregnant," Mal said, voice soothing. "That means he never wanted to marry you or start a family. He doesn't deserve your tears."

"He just has a lot going on right now."

Van stole a cookie. "Rule one, sweetheart. Never make excuses for someone's mistreatment of you. No matter what he has going on, yelling at you and calling you names isn't right."

Mal nodded. "When you're in a relationship with someone, you both should be absolutely honest about what you want. This man said one thing, but clearly wanted something else. How did you spend most of your time together?"

Bianca's face turned red. "It wasn't just about sex."

"There's our answer." Mal sighed.

Bianca was quiet for a while. She ate her cookies and drank her cocoa, clearly exhausted.

"How far along are you?" Van asked, breaking the silence.

"Three months." Bianca bundled back into the blanket. "He doesn't want the baby. I can't raise a kid all by myself. What am I going to do Mom?"

"Think about what *you* want," Van answered. "Spend a little time imagining yourself raising a baby while going to high school and college, because you're going to college. You have options, but it is your choice. If you want an abortion Mal and I will drive you to the clinic ourselves. If you want the child, I'm right here."

"*We're* right here," Mal corrected. "I can stay in Hobson Hills as long as you need me to. I love kids."

"Options," Bianca whispered. "What options do I really

have? I don't want an abortion. I don't want to raise the baby without its father."

"Then adoption." Van hugged her. "We can find a nice couple to adopt the baby."

Bianca nodded, looking relieved. "Yeah, I like that idea."

With somewhat of a plan, Bianca quickly fell asleep on the couch. Van and Mal went to his room, shutting the door behind them. Truffle looked up, glaring at them for waking him from his nap.

"I'm so angry," Van said, voice low. "I want this man in jail for taking advantage of my daughter. I want to scream at her for dating an older man, a married man, a man with fucking kids. I also want to scream at him for breaking her heart. Damn it, Mal. What are we going to do?"

Mal hugged her. "Exactly what we told Bianca. We're going to be here for her and support the choices she makes about the baby. However, as soon as we know who the man is, we will file charges. I don't care how old he is. He's clearly a predator."

Van nodded. "Yes. We'll do that." She gave him a relieved look. "I'm glad you're here."

"I'm glad you invited me to be part of your family." He smiled softly. "I'll stay here with you all. Cain will be living here anyway. It's time I settle down, especially when my best friend and the daughter of my heart need me."

"Is Cain coming this weekend?"

Mal winced. "He won't be coming back until the trial is over. The villains have people following him, and he doesn't want to lead them to Roe."

"Go see him." Van patted his back. "We'll take care of Betty and Truffle. Go see him this weekend. You both need it."

"Are you sure?"

"Yes." She eyed him. "Do you know who Bianca thinks the best father in the entire world is?"

"Marco or Bennett Wilson?"

She shook her head. "You. She thinks you are the absolute best. Who do think she will want to adopt the baby?"

His eyes widened and he pointed at himself. "Me?"

"Just be prepared if she asks. Talk to Cain."

Mal grabbed his phone. "I'll book a flight now."

ain shuffled the papers in front of him, looking for the forms he needed. Working from home wasn't ideal, but they wouldn't let him back in the office after he'd worked ten days in a row. Now, he was forced to lounge on his couch as he reviewed Roe's case for the umpteenth time. If Mal was here, he would have snacks and delicious tea made with fresh foraged herbs.

The house was suddenly echoingly empty. If Mal was there, music would fill the kitchen as the omega gracefully dodged Betty to move from the stove to the cabinets. Maybe he would still be working on the couch, but Truffle would be sprawled on his lap, purring loudly.

A buzz sounded loudly, signaling someone at the downstairs.

Cain frowned, then went to the door and spoke into the speaker. "Benson residence."

"Hey," a sing song voice came through.

A grin slowly spread across his face. "Mal?"

"Yep."

He quickly unlocked the door. "Third floor, apartment B."

A few moments later and Mal was in his arms, head resting on top of Cain's. It was the first time he had dated someone taller than him, but he liked it. His lanky frame was perfect. Completely and utterly perfect.

"I'm going to be a daddy," Mal said.

Cain's eyes widened and he leaned back. "Betty is too young to have babies. Did Truffle knock some cat up? I thought he was neutered."

"Bianca is pregnant," Mal blurted out, looking exhausted. "She won't tell us who the father is, but we now know he is married with children and he broke up with her."

"Married? How old is he?" Cain scowled, anger growing in his gut. "He's going to jail. I don't care if he's eighteen and close to her age. If he's married with kids, then he's much more experienced than Bianca and manipulated her. Statutory rape at the very least."

"I don't think he's close to her age." Mal sniffled. "He groomed her. She said he told her not to tell anyone about them being together because they wouldn't understand, especially her mom. He isolated her and lied to her. Then he abandoned her when she told him she's pregnant."

"God, she's pregnant." Cain groaned. "She's too young."

"That's why she asked me to adopt the baby." Mal's smile was strained. "She says she'll make a better big sister than a mother right now."

Cain rubbed his face, then pulled Mal back into his arms. "So, we are going to be fathers? My mother will be happy."

"We?" Mal's eyes lit with hope. "You don't want to break up with me?"

Cain arched a brow. "Do you doubt me?"

"You know I can't resist the eyebrow." Mal snuggled closer. "Okay, I feel a lot better."

"I'm glad you are here, but you know we can't do this often, right? They have people watching me."

"Stupid villains are cockblocking me."

Cain nuzzled his neck. "I love you."

Mal squeaked and squeezed him tightly, kissing the top of his head. "I love you too. Oh, geez. I planned this whole thing for the next D&D game night. I was going to rescue you from a direwolf. Then when you said thanks, I was going to say that it was only right to save you since I love you. It was going to be awesome. Rick and the others will be disappointed."

"They'll survive." Cain slipped to his knees, suddenly needing to be closer to Mal. He wanted to taste him, to feel him in every way.

"Cain?" Mal asked, squeaking again when Cain unbuttoned his shorts.

He pulled Mal's hardening dick from his underwear and stroked him, admiring the sight of his omega. Cain sucked one of Mal's heavy balls into his mouth, and his omega groaned, hands grasping Cain's head. He stroked Mal's very hard length, then swirled his tongue around the head of his dick.

Mal squeezed Cain's head, gripping his short hair, so Cain changed his angle, taking more of Mal's dick into his mouth. He thoroughly enjoyed it when Mal's hands tightened. Seeing the omega out of control was Cain's new favorite thing.

Cain felt Mal's muscles tense, and a second later he happily drank the omega's release. Cain was a gentleman, so he allowed Mal a full thirty seconds to recover before he stood up.

"Want inside you." He spun Mal around, pinning him to the wall. "Is this okay?" His hands cupped Mal's ass almost reverently.

"Yep," Mal said, voice gruff. "I'm good. Let's go. Get inside me already."

Cain chuckled and lowered to his knees again. He placed several tiny, gentle bites on each cheek of Mal's ass. Then he slid his fingers through Mal's crease and found his hole. Using the pack of lube Mal suddenly handed him, he slowly stretched Mal's ass, one finger, then two, then three.

Mal moaned and pushed back, riding Cain's fingers.

After a moment, Cain stood and nibbled the back of Mal's neck. "I love you so much." He bit down gently, then thrust into Mal's ass.

Mal cried out and arched his back as Cain pounded into him.

Cain gripped Mal's hips and lifted him half off his feet, angling his body so his dick hit just the right spot to drive his omega mad.

"Oh, damn. Right there." Mal panted. "Don't come, don't come, don't come."

The chanting didn't work. Cain keep steady stroked against Mal's prostate, and he came all over the entryway wall.

Cain didn't last much longer. He grunted and held Mal still as he came, filling the omega's ass.

"That feels so good," Mal said, forehead pressed to the wall. "Wait, that feels good. Dang it, we forgot to use a condom. I'm not on any birth control."

Cain grunted and slowly lowered Mal to his feet and wrapped his arms around him. "It's alright. We're together. If you get pregnant, then you get pregnant. We'll be safe next time."

Mal snorted. "So blithe. Can you imagine having a newborn and being pregnant at the same time? I can and it's not fun."

Cain fought a smile. He loved the idea of Mal round with his child. However, he wanted to keep his balls, so he would not say that aloud.

~

THE NEXT MORNING, sunlight was only beginning to fill the sky when Mal woke up. He stretched his body, smiling at the delicious aches that reminded him of each and every intimate moment with the man he loved. His dick stirred at the memory.

He leaned over and buried his face in the crook of Cain's neck, moving his naked body closer to the warmth of his alpha. His ass was still a bit tender from the night before, but there were other ways to satisfy his hunger. *This is my man,* he thought, joy bubbling through him.

With all the stress of the past few days, being with Cain was a balm to his soul. Mal wasn't alone. Van and Bianca and him weren't alone. They were a strange found family that would be added to Mal's family forest. It was only proper that a Reed gained a family like that.

Mal playfully licked and nipped Cain's neck while one hand strolled south to stroke Cain's long, thick dick to life. His alpha was generously endowed and Mal had never been so grateful.

Cain moaned and his sleepy brown eyes opened. "Love?"

"I like that term of endearment. Much better than weirdo." Mal kissed him softly, then pushed the covers back. "Can I?"

Cain smiled sleepily and raised his hands over his head. "Absolutely."

Mal trailed his lips down Cain's lightly haired chest, one hand kneading the muscles a lawyer shouldn't have. He bit a nipple, then licked it before doing the same to the other one. Mal took his time pressing kisses to Cain's slightly soft stomach.

"Ignore the paunch," Cain said, breathing heavily.

"Why would I ignore any delicious part of you?" Mal kissed his stomach again. "I love every inch of you."

When his mouth reached Cain's dick, Mal hummed in pleasure. He stroked Cain's length, base to tip, then sat up and started working his alpha's dick, licking his lips when he saw precum drip from the tip.

Mal leaned down and swallowed the head, sucking gently, while he stroked the rest of Cain's hard length. Steadily, he took more and more of Cain's dick in his mouth, sucking hard as he went.

Cain's hands gently cupped Mal's head. He looked up, enjoying the sight of his alpha's face flushed with arousal.

Mal pressed his own dick against the bed, hips moving in rhythm with his strokes. He worked Mal's dick for a while, then moved onto his balls, sucking first one, then the other into his mouth.

"Fuck, Mal!" Cain's grip on his head tightened, then he was spurting between them. Mal barely closed his eyes in time.

Cain panted as he grabbed the sheet, wiping at Mal's face. "I'm so sorry."

Mal stifled a giggle and rolled over. "Finish me?"

Cain's eyes grew heavy, and he looked very pleased at the sight of Mal's hard dick. "With pleasure."

CHAPTER 11

I am the king of sneak, Mal told himself as he took photos with his phone. No one noticed him hunched behind the stall for Abel's brewery. He was a ninja. The Hobson Hills Summer Festival was in full swing, and people were having fun. Children and adults alike ran from ride to ride, and each food and drink stall had a long queue.

Mal blended in perfectly. Yes, maybe he appeared a little creepy, but Sheriff McKenzie and Roe were kissing. It was too good an opportunity to waste. Cain would want to see this. *I miss him so much,* he thought, suddenly wanting to cry. It had been two weeks since he'd last seen him. Cain should be there with him, sneaking to take pictures of his friend's important moment. It was clear Roe liked Sheriff McKenzie and the older man certainly returned those feelings. This kiss was their first and a declaration of their feelings. *Cain should be here.*

He snapped another picture and smiled sadly. "Good job, Roe. Cain would be proud."

"Are you sending those to Cain?" A deep voice sounded from behind him.

Mal shrieked, jumping and spinning around all at once.

A large, muscular, bald man stood behind him. Wally – Roe's bodyguard.

Pressing his hand to his heart, Mal took deep breaths. "You scared the crap out of me."

Wally smirked and handed Mal a slip of paper. "Tell Cain I said hello." He started walking back to Roe's group.

"What is this?" Mal asked, scratching his itchy stomach. It had been irritating him over the last few weeks.

Wally looked over his shoulder. "The address to the house Cain just bought. You should check out the kitchen."

Mal pressed his hands to his warm cheeks. Cain really did it. He said he was going to move there, and he had bought a house. Grandpa David was going to be so mad, but Mal needed to settle down in Hobson Hills. The baby would need to be near Van and Bianca. Cain would need to be near his dad so they could open their bait shop. Not that Cain or his father had any idea they were going to open a bait shop, but the town needed a new one.

Old Shakey owned the best little bait shop near one of the lakes around Hobson Hills. He handed out fishing tips along with a variety of different worms and insects. The old beta was past the point of retirement. Cain and his dad needed to buy the shop and run it. Shakey could hang around and talk to the customers without having to do any of the hard work.

"What are you dreaming about, young'un?" an amused voice asked.

Startled, Mal looked up, eyes widening as he realized who it was. "Oh, shit."

Gramps Wilson leaned out of the back of Abel's stall. His blue eyes and soft smile were kind and gentle, instantly making Mal's eyes water as a surge of homesickness hit him.

"Haven't seen you around, but I've heard about you," Gramps said, laughing. "You don't dodge cameras as well as you think, but Noah was real impressed with your moonwalk dance. His kids were more impressed with the toys you and your friends left in the stalls. Laurel and I enjoy your pranks. The grandkids deserve it." Gramps scratched his chin. "Oh, and Abel's dogs were impressed with the doggy toy beers you filled his desk with, but I was a bit confused. I understand the toy beers at the brewery, but why were there some toy bears in there too?"

"Miscommunication with my minions." Mal shuffled his feet, turning in circles while he tried to figure out what to do. "Oh, geez."

Gramps laughed. "You look just like my daddy did when he got caught doing some mischief." His eyes narrowed as he studied Mal. "You actually look a lot like my daddy. What's your name, son?"

"M…Malcolm."

"Really? That was my daddy's name."

"Oh, geez. Oh, geez. Oh, geez. I have to go." Mal stopped circling and ran for the festival exit. He tucked the slip of paper that Wally had given him away, then called his grandpa while he ran.

"About time you called," David Reed said, deep voice rough. "It's been two whole months. I thought you were dead in a ditch."

"You thought I was dead in a ditch, but you didn't bother trying to call me or at least alert the police?" Mal asked, offended despite the trouble he was about to bring to his grandpa.

"Eh, I'm old. Thought I'd see you soon enough in the afterlife."

Mal rolled his eyes. All of his grandparents were in really good health considering their age.

"What's happening? You called for a reason." David sounded amused. "I'm still mad that you're seeing that

Benson boy. Next thing you know, you'll be visiting Wilsons."

"GrampsWilsontalkedtomeandsaidIlookedlikehisdad," Mal said, words running together. "Oh, geez. Please don't be mad at me. I avoided the Wilsons. I swear I did. He just popped out of a festival stall. Who does that? People shouldn't sneak up on others. They need to respect boundaries and anonymity."

"Not sure that's something you have the right to say," David said, sounding amused. "Considering all those pranks you play on the Wilsons."

"Maybe this is a good thing." Mal's voice sounded desperate, even to his own ears. "You could finally talk to him. Explain everything. The Wilsons are good people, Grandpa. I promise. Plus, Cain bought a house here. In Hobson Hills. He wants to raise the baby with me."

"Baby?" David's voice turned cold. "Did that boy get you pregnant? He better want to help you raise the baby."

"I'm an adult, Grandpa. Of course, we used protection." *Well, except for the first time,* he reminded himself. *Grandpa doesn't need to know that. I'm practically thirty. I know what I'm doing.* Feeling better, he continued. "The daughter of my heart is the one that's pregnant. She wants me to adopt the baby."

"That sweet girl you talk about all the time?" David sounded even angrier. "She's a child. Who the hell got her in that situation?"

"She won't say." Mal felt slightly bad for using Bianca to turn the conversation away from his own confession. "I need to be here for her."

"Of course, you do." David sighed. "Maybe it is time to talk to Gerard Wilson. If you're settling there with that Benson boy, then I better clear the air. You look just like that picture of my daddy. There's no way he won't put it together."

Mal let out a large sigh of relief and scratched his itchy stomach. It had been bothering him all week. "Thank you, Grandpa. I'm sorry that it's my fault you have to do this now."

"It's something I should have done a long time ago." David sighed. "The way you talk about that family makes me want to get to know them. Though with all the trouble you cause them, they will probably disown you as soon as they know about you."

"Worth it." Mal shrugged and hopped into the truck. It was time to go home and make plans. But first, he would take a look at the house Cain had bought.

He drove to the address on the slip of paper Wally had given him, jaw dropping at the sight of the beautiful two-story home. It sat close to Mal's favorite lake, the one Old Shakey's bait shop served. It was a mix of stone and wood, with a wraparound porch and a large, attached garage. The yard was expansive and bordered one of the many state parks that Mal was allowed to forage in.

"Wow." He walked around the house, peeking in the windows and admiring the sunroom. "Holy shit, this kitchen is huge. I can make so many videos."

Mal could easily envision himself in this house with Cain by his side. They would be good parents, and he already knew Cain was the perfect partner in mischief-making. Plus, Mal could finally allow himself to say it and think it – he loved Cain. The alpha was his future.

THE SUN WAS SINKING below the trees by the time that Mal arrived back at his RV. All thoughts of Cain's house and his grandpa's upcoming call disappeared at the sight that awaited him. Bianca sat on the steps with Betty, trembling. Her knees were raised, and her head was pressed against them. Her long, brown hair fell in tangled knots, and her clothes were covered in dirt.

Mal hurried and knelt in front of her, panic pushing everything from his mind. "What's wrong, sweetheart? Are you hurt? Is Van okay?"

She slowly raised her head, and he flinched. Her face was bruised and bloody, eyes already swelling. "Mal," she whispered, voice full of pain.

"Who did this?" he asked, hands shaking with the rage building inside him. He gently brushed her hair back from her face. "Who hurt you, Bianca?"

"Doesn't matter." She shuddered and fell against him. "He kicked Betty."

The piglet stared up at him, seemingly completely undamaged, but concerned about her second favorite human.

He wrapped his arms around Bianca as she sobbed. "We need to get you to a hospital. The county one is what? Forty minutes away? I should call an ambulance."

"No, please. I can't go there." She drew in a wet breath. "Please just call Mom. Please."

Against his better judgment, Mal gave in and quickly dialed Van's number. His friend was working at the hospital.

"Mal?" Van asked, taking the call. "This better be more important than a request to bring you junk food for a late-night snack."

"Van, it's an emergency. Come to the RV now."

He hung up before she could respond. There was no point in telling her anything until she got there.

Scooping Bianca into his arms, he gently carried her into the RV, mentally cursing the narrow door. Betty trotted behind them, then went to inspect her food bowl. He set his daughter down on the couch, then ran for his first aid kit.

"Where's it hurt, angel?"

"My face, my arms," she mumbled, leaning against the couch pillow. She held Truffle in her arms. The cat purred loudly, offering comfort the best way he knew how. "I think I sprained my ankle too."

Mal checked her over, happy to see nothing looked broken. She had clearly been punched more than once and someone had grabbed her hard, leaving large bruises on her arms.

"Once your mom gets here, we need to bring you to the hospital, okay? I'm not an expert at this."

"I don't want to."

"We aren't giving you a choice. This is one benefit from being an adult. We get to make the important decisions."

"Are you an adult?" she asked, looking pitiful.

Mal snorted, trying not to be offended. "Don't let my laid-back exterior fool you, my dear. While emotional maturity is an ongoing journey, I'm self-aware and take responsibility for my actions. Plus, I know the difference between needs and wants. In my mind, those are the most important aspects of adulthood."

"I'm an adult. I take care of myself and definitely know the difference between needs and wants. I'm not stupid."

"What do you think you need to do right now?" he asked gently.

Bianca looked confused. "What?"

"When I say needs and wants, I don't mean that you know you need food, water, and shelter. You need to know the difference between what you need to do and what you want to do. You *need* to go to the hospital. You seem to *want* to ignore whatever is happening here, hoping it will go away."

"I don't want to think about it." She leaned her head on his shoulder. "It's my choice not to go to the hospital."

"Nope. That's Van's decision. Mine too if you accept me as your dad."

She started crying again. "I want you to be my dad. I don't want to think about this. About what he did. About the baby. What am I supposed to do, Mal?"

"You're young, Bianca," he said softly. "Leave all the worrying to us. You aren't alone."

"I'm not a good person," she whispered. "I did something bad. Real bad."

"You're one of the best people I know. Good people make poor choices sometimes." He kissed the top of her head. "Don't worry about it. We'll take care of it no matter what."

She started crying again and he held her as she sobbed. They sat like that until Van arrived, banging the door open as she ran in.

Mal left them alone to talk and went to his room. He sent a message to cancel the evening yoga session and searched for hospitals further away. Since Bianca wouldn't go to the county hospital, they needed to go further out.

More than an hour passed, but it felt so much longer. Mal couldn't settle the anger growing in him. Bianca was so young. Someone had hurt her. Someone had purposely hit that sweet child.

A few moments later, Van slipped into his room, shutting the door behind her.

"Paula is with her right now." Her face was haggard, and she had clearly been crying. "I need a favor, Mal."

"Anything." He stopped pacing and grabbed her hand. "Is she alright? Who did that to her?"

Van shook her head. "Don't worry about that. I need you to take Bianca away from Hobson Hills for a while. At least six months. Stay in Maine, but she needs to go to a hospital to get checked out. It looks like nothing's broken, but I'm not an expert. Then, she'll need to see a good obstetrician."

"Obstetrician?" he asked, confused. "Why?"

"She's three months pregnant," Van reminded him, voice breaking. "The father doesn't matter. He's a piece of shit. She needs us."

"He's the one that hit her." Mal started pacing again, mind processing everything.

"He. Doesn't. Matter." Van pulled him to a stop. "Mal, my girl needs somewhere safe to recuperate. The trash that put her in this position doesn't matter. I don't need anger from you. She doesn't need that. We need your love."

Mal took a deep breath and held it before slowly exhaling. He did it again, then again, forcefully pushing the rage away so he could focus on what was beneath it. He loved Van and Bianca like family. They needed him to be strong. Van was right. Nothing else mattered right then.

"Okay." He nodded. "I'll take care of her, Van."

"Thank you." She looked relieved and tired.

He pulled her into a hug, knowing this wasn't easy on her. "Everything will be okay. I promise."

As he waited for Van to return with some of Bianca's clothes, he video called Cain. It was late, but he knew his alpha would answer.

"Mal?" Cain looked sleepy. He was clearly in bed, his chest bare and his hair tousled.

His alpha was there, looking at him, a comfort even if he was several states away. Mal couldn't keep the tears at bay. He cried as he explained the situation.

Emotions flew across Cain's face – worry, anger, sadness, determination. "I'll get the paperwork together for you to have temporary guardianship of Bianca. That way she can be homeschooled and stay caught up with her studies while you two are away."

Mal nodded, wiping his eyes. "Thank you, love. I don't know what I would do without you."

Cain looked torn. "I want to come to you right now."

"No." Mal shook his head. "This is enough. Roe needs you there. Plus, it could be dangerous, remember?"

Rage filled the alpha's face for a moment before he forced it away. "You're my heart, Mal. I should be with you." He held up a hand before Mal could protest. "I acknowledge that you're right. I have to stay here. However, I am not happy about it."

Mal heard the door to the RV open and close. "I need to go. We're leaving out tonight. I'll let you know where we end up."

"I love you," Cain said with a sigh. "You are a good dad."

Mal let the warmth of his words fill him. He knew Cain loved him. He could see it right there on the man's face. It was nice to hear the words, though.

"I love you too."

CHAPTER 12

OCTOBER

"*R*elax and stretch into child pose." Mal demonstrated for the camera. "Knees on the mat, toes touching. Remember to widen your knees as much as possible but keep it comfortable. Don't hurt yourself trying to keep up with Bom." Chuckles sounded from the smart screen of the television. He breathed out as he folded his body down, enjoying the relief on his back.

Lately, he was feeling more achy than usual. Probably because of the creature growing inside him. Last month he had concluded that he couldn't keep ignoring the nausea, fatigue, and frequent bathroom trips. He had gone to the doctor and confirmed the most inconvenient news. He was pregnant.

He let his breath out and cleared his mind. "Five breaths here. Ground yourself, clear your mind. It's time for some self-reflection. Check-in."

Mal watched the others on the screen. Okay, he watched Cain. His alpha looked stressed and struggled to relax. The case was coming to a head. Roe had been attacked while taking his son to his first semester of college. Sheriff

102

McKenzie had been hurt. However, one good thing came from the incident. They had the contract criminal behind bars, and he was willing to testify against, not only the Dorsey couple, but also the Loriston police.

Then there was Mal's news. Cain wanted to be with Mal, especially since both Mal and Bianca were pregnant, but there was still a contract out on him. Until the trial was over, Cain wasn't safe. Even being around Cain wasn't safe. James and Gabriel Dorsey weren't focused on Roe anymore. They wanted the threat of Cain and Jasper removed.

Mal forced the thoughts from his mind and focused on the session he led. He slowly talked them through the last bit, then joined the group in a long *om*.

As the session ended, Tripp stood up, grinning. "Why, Mal, you're practically glowing. Any news you would like to share?"

Mal rolled his eyes. "Who told you?"

Cain winced. "That would be me. Sorry, love. It slipped out when I was talking investments with him."

"Slipped out?" Tripp snickered, brain like a twelve-year-old.

"Mal, are you pregnant?" Bom asked, studying him closely.

"You poor thing." Marta gave him a sympathetic look. The newest addition to her family was still causing her nipples pain. And keeping the whole household awake at night. And worrying them by catching a cold over the weekend. Babies were a lot of work.

He cleared his throat. "Yes, everyone. I am pregnant. Starting next week, Cain will help me lead the group. Basically, I'll talk and he'll demonstrate the poses for those of you that need a visual."

"How are the new pregnancy yoga sessions going?" Cain asked, eyes practically devouring him through the screen.

"More sessions?" Marta and Bom instantly perked up.

Mal chuckled. "You can join if you would like. Info is on my website. It's just a gentle session in the late morning for pregnant folks. Good prenatal care. Bianca helps me lead it." He blew a kiss to Cain. "To answer your question, it's going well. There are three members so far. Besides Bia and I."

His friends said goodbye one by one and signed out leaving him with Cain.

"How is Bianca doing?"

"I'm okay." The teen poked her head into view of the camera. "Doing homework in the kitchen with Truffle and Betty." She walked into view, showing off an impressive baby bump. "I have no privacy. Mal makes me eat healthy stuff, and we go foraging every day. Now he has me doing prenatal yoga too." She sighed. "I miss junk food and reality shows, but my grades have never been better. Teddy is doing well too."

They had found out she was having a boy, so Cain and Mal had named him Theodore David Reed. Teddy for short.

Cain smiled warmly. "I am very happy the two of you are doing well. Have you decided on a university yet?"

"I told you already," she answered, snorting a laugh. "There is no way my grades are good enough for a scholarship. I'm going to have to work and save for a year before starting."

Cain's eyes narrowed. "I told you already that I am paying for your tuition. You will be my daughter one day soon. It is my joy to help you in any way I can."

"The two of you are so stubborn." Bianca groaned and sat on the couch. "You aren't even married to Mal yet."

"If you like it, then you should have put a ring on it." Mal did his best Beyonce and danced while singing. Betty joined him, grunting as she ran around him.

Cain smirked. "Give me time, and I'll finally have you where I want you, weirdo."

Bianca fake gagged. "You two are worse than Mom and Mark. Paula says they're totally gross now that they're dating. I'm almost happy to be crammed in an RV with Mal. That is until you two start sweet-talking one another."

"One day, you'll be a gross adult and will find someone to flirt with until it makes Teddy and his little sibling gag." Mal rubbed his own very small baby bump.

She rolled her eyes and lay on her side, placing a pillow between her knees. "Can we have salmon tonight?"

"Oh, with lentils and leeks." Mal mentally went through what ingredients he had. "Yep."

The three of them talked for another hour, enjoying each other's presence even though Cain was far away. One day soon, they would be together again.

He couldn't wait and could already envision them in the new house's kitchen. Van and Mark would sit at the bar, cuddled together. Paula and Bianca would be in the living room, watching some clearly scripted reality show about living on a super yacht. Cain would be at the small table in the corner of the kitchen with Teddy and a little blurry faced baby. He'd probably be feeding them or reading them law books. Something serious like that.

Mal would be exactly where he wanted to be. Cooking for the people he loved.

CHAPTER 13

MARCH

"On the charge of solicitation of murder, the jury finds both James and Gabriel Dorsey guilty," the court clerk read aloud.

Cain held his breath. That wasn't the most important charge.

"On the charge of attempted murder, the jury finds both James and Gabriel Dorsey guilty."

The crowd of friends and family gathered behind them cheered. The clerk continued reading, but Cain didn't hear. He pulled Roe from his seat and hugged his friend. The omega was several months pregnant but had still made the trip from Maine to Georgia to attend the trial.

"We got them," Roe said, voice cracking.

"Yes, we did. Well, Jasper did most of the work, but we helped," Cain said, grinning. Fortunately, the judge had allowed the two men to be tried together. Only one trial for Roe to attend was more than enough. Cain and Jasper had agreed to forgo pressing charges for the contracts placed on their own lives. They both wanted this done and over. Jasper had just found out he was pregnant and wanted to focus on his career and family. Cain wanted to be with Mal and Teddy.

"Guilty on all charges," Jasper said, smirking. "The sentence will be a minimum of five years in prison. Minimum."

"It should be more," Roe said, sniffling. "I'm so happy this is over."

Cain nodded, as he let Roe go. The man they had hired to kill Roe, Bollinger, had made a deal with investigators, so he was only sentenced to five years. Likely James and Gabriel would get at least ten years.

Ian McKenzie, Roe's fiancé, wrapped an arm around Roe's shoulders and pulled him into his arms. "No more worrying about that trash anymore. You're free of them."

Roe wiped his face, but the tears kept falling. "Why can't I stop crying. God, this is good news."

"After years of being hunted by those bastards, the relief must be unreal." Cain shook his head. "Go home, Roe. Hug the kids and get some rest. You don't have to worry about this shit anymore."

Roe pulled Cain and Jasper into a group hug. "Thank you for sticking with me through all this. I know it wasn't easy."

Cain frowned, remembering the day Roe had come to the law firm, shaken and scared. The omega's family had been friends with Cain's parents, but that wasn't why he'd taken the case. James and Gabriel had done everything they could to isolate the omega and his children. James had wanted Roe's family's business, and Gabriel had wanted to get rid of Roe permanently.

Cain had known if his firm didn't help Roe, no one would. Gabriel had a way of charming everyone he met. At the time, he had already ruined Roe socially and had even gotten the police to ignore Roe's complaints about being stalked and harassed.

"It's done," Jasper said, eying Cain. "Are you really going to leave Atlanta now?"

Cain nodded. "The firm is in good hands, and I'm ready."

McKenzie slapped his shoulder. "We drove past the house you bought the other day. Isn't it a bit too big for you?"

"I looked through the window," Roe said, wiping his eyes again. "Why do you need a kitchen that size? You don't cook."

"You could always ask for a key and go inside," Cain pointed out, ignoring their questions.

He couldn't really explain what led him to buy the large house across the lake from his parents without telling them about Mal, Teddy, and the daughter they would have in another few months. Considering he hadn't told his parents or brothers yet, that would be a bad idea.

It had been months since he'd seen Mal in person. Their calls and the short moments in between yoga sessions were barely sustaining him. He had watched every single cooking episode on Mal's channel more times than he wanted to admit. Cain needed the omega in the same room as him, talking to Cain, brightening the room with his laughter. He wanted to care for his pregnant omega. To rug his feet and pamper him in every way possible.

Cain shook his body, rolling his shoulders back. Tension disappeared and excitement took its place. He was finally going home. He could picture himself sitting in the light-filled kitchen, Mal moving about, describing some ridiculous prank he pulled on a Wilson while cooking one of the *simple* meals that weren't actually simple to make. It was time for his happily ever after.

TWO DAYS LATER, Cain sat on his very own dock, wrapped in a thick coat, poorly knitted scarf, and an odd, knitted penguin hat that was too big for any child to wear. He had forgotten how cold Maine was. Spring was warmer than winter, but still much colder than Georgia. His parents and brothers sat with him, each one much better prepared for the weather. He noticed none of them had to wear a knitted penguin hat.

"You have a newborn son and a daughter on the way," John Benson, his father, repeated, face slack with shock. "They've been in Maine and you've been in Georgia for months."

Susan Benson, his mother, looked just as shocked. "Why are we only hearing about this now? Frank told us you were dating someone, but that was months ago. This is what we get for giving you space."

Cain winced. "I wanted to tell you in person, but I was stuck in Atlanta. The Dorseys had a contract on me, so I did not want any of you to be in danger. The man they hired is in jail now, awaiting his own trial. Jasper will handle that of course."

"A contract," John echoed, voice rising. "Son, what were you thinking. That's why you missed the holidays, isn't it? Why didn't you say anything. That kind of situation is exactly when you need your family around you."

Cain shrugged. "I had a bodyguard."

"He had a bodyguard," Carter, his brother, said mockingly. "Would the bodyguard have kept you company and supported you while you went through this?"

Puzzled, Cain arched a brow. "Well, that is not what I paid him to do, so probably not."

Caden, Cain's other brother, placed a hand on Carter's arm, keeping the younger man in his seat. "The important thing is that you are here now."

"Why didn't you bring Robin and Suzie?" Cain asked, fighting a pout. "I specifically asked you to bring them."

"Suzie and Yeo are sleeping, and Robin is with his other grandparents. You will have to wait for cuddle time. I will put you on the schedule." Caden sighed. "Linc, will you please hug your uncle? He has cuddle withdraws."

Caden's eldest, Lincoln, was the only child there today. The young boy sat at the end of the dock with a fishing pole, swinging his feet.

"Sure." Linc set his pole down and ran to Cain. "I'll hug you, Uncle Cain."

Cain pulled the boy in for a tight hug, then stood and spun him in circles, enjoying his giggles. "That is exactly what I needed."

After Linc was back to fishing, Susan gave Cain a hard look. "Maybe we could not have been there for you, Cain, but we could have been there for your omega."

Cain winced. "It is more complicated than you know. Teddy is our adopted son. His mother is a young teen named Bianca. Mal loves her like a daughter and is taking care of her right now as she recovers from some traumatic events."

"We could have been there for them both," Susan said sadly. "You should not shut family out, Cain. We all learned that with Carter. Remember?"

Guilt shot through Cain, making his stomach gurgle. "I'm sorry, Mom. You are right."

Carter sighed. "Cain's been alone in Atlanta for a while now. Once you get used to relying on yourself, it's hard to bring other people back in. Like Caden said. The important thing is that Cain is here now. While your house is impressive, it doesn't have a nursery. I think you'll need help with that, right?"

Cain nodded, thankful for the distraction Carter had just given him. "Yes. Mom, can you help me with the nursery? Mal and the kids will be coming home in a couple of weeks. Dad, Mal loves to fish, and I need to learn more about it. For some reason he thinks You and I are going to open a bait shop? I do not like bugs, but if it will make him happy, then I will at least consider it."

Carter and Caden both laughed.

"You? Open a bait shop?" Carter asked, snickering.

"You wouldn't even swat a spider when you were a kid. You always made Mom come and do it." Caden grinned.

Susan sighed. "Why does your omega want you to open a bait shop?"

"I said *Dad and I*," he corrected, waving to his dad. "He says 'Old Shakey' needs to retire, and Dad and I should spend more time together. How that leads to a bait shop, I am not sure. It is not my place to question."

John rubbed his chin. "Old Shakey is having problems with his arthritis. His shop is the best around too. Has a good reputation and a quality supply chain."

"According to Mal, the only other option is to open our own law firm," Cain said, shrugging. "Or I can come up with my own ideas of what to do with my time."

"That's too much work." John grinned. "I need to talk to Old Shakey. I think I'm going to like your omega, Cain. Good job."

Cain wrinkled his nose. "Why can't we open a small law office?"

"Did that already." John waved his concern away. "I want something new, and I like the idea of a running a bait shop with my son."

Carter and Caden gave him sympathetic looks.

Cain sighed. It appeared that he would need to grow accustomed to the idea of bugs.

CHAPTER 14

"The oatcakes I make are sweetened and are more like cookies or biscuits than cake. They use oats and eggs, all good stuff for a recuperating new parent." Mal kissed the top of Teddy's head and checked the oatcakes in the oven. The newborn stayed with Mal as much as possible. At the moment, he slept in the newborn sling Mal wore, his curly brown hair the only thing in view of the cameras.

"Postnatal care is just as important as prenatal care. It speeds your recovery and helps your overall wellbeing. Plus, if you are breastfeeding, then it even helps nourish your newborn." Noting the nice brown color, Mal took the pan out of the oven and quickly moved each oatcake to the cooling rack.

"I'm going to let these cool, then add some fresh berries and diced mango and banana to half of them. Bianca likes sweet oatcakes, but you can also make them a little more savory by adding scrambled eggs and avocado slices. You can also just eat them as is or with jam. These are Canadian oatcakes rather than Scottish, so they're already sweet. That means savory for me, so I'm going to add egg, avocado, and a bit of parsley to mine."

Mal took his time gathering the ingredients to top the oatcakes, explaining the good and bad qualities of each for the camera. Then he topped each oatcake a little differently, making sure the camera caught as much footage as possible. It always took him forever to film an episode and edit it. He discovered early on that getting as much footage as possible was the best way to avoid having to refilm anything. He had videos as short as thirty seconds and as long as an hour, but they all needed footage.

By the time he had finished filming and set the small bar table, Bianca was stirring. It had only been a month since she had given birth to Teddy, but it felt like ages had passed. She seemed happier and more at peace with herself.

She yawned as she crawled out of the sofa bed. "That smells really good."

"Eat up, sweetheart. Are you sure about today?"

"I'm ready to see Mom and Paula again." Bianca smiled at him, then tucked into her food.

They were going home today. Van and Bianca both had okayed the idea. Mal still wasn't sure why Bianca had needed to leave Hobson Hills in the first place, but to each their own. He still held hopes that Bianca would let the name of the birth father slip so Mal could send Cain after him. So far, she had remained silent about it.

Teddy gurgled, waking up. He blinked his big brown eyes a couple of times, and Mal fell in love all over again. He loved this little boy as much as he would love his own blood once the little monster was born. Teddy had been an angel for Bianca. However, his daughter was already practicing to be a professional soccer player. She had the talent too.

Mal was happy they were returning to Hobson Hills mostly because Cain had made the permanent move a few days ago. His alpha was working on the nursery for Teddy and their monster baby. Soon, there would be more space for everyone, Mal included.

Pulling Bianca into a hug, he tried to squeeze as much love and gratitude into their embrace as he could without squashing Teddy. "Thank you for letting me be a part of your life. I love you and am so happy you're my daughter."

The teen sniffled and hugged him back. "I love you too. I don't know what I would do without you. Thank you for supporting me, Mal. Adulting is hard, and thanks to you, I got to put it off a little longer."

"You promise you'll keep up with the therapy appointments even if I'm not there to push you?" He swayed back and forth, enjoying the hug.

"I promise. Mom even signed me up to visit the counselor at Noah Wilson's horse ranch. You remember the one we broke into?"

"I don't recall that at all. You must be confusing me for someone else."

Bianca snorted a laugh. "Trust me. There's no one else like you. Now, you have to let me go if you want to drive us home."

He groaned. "I don't wanna."

"You said adults have to do things they don't want too sometimes. Remember?"

"Yeah, yeah. Why do you listen so well?"

"Because you keep talking until I do. Otherwise, I'd never get you to hush."

AFTER ARRIVING IN HOBSON HILLS, Mal left Bianca and Teddy with Van and headed home. *Home*, he thought, excitement building. It had been a long time since a place had been home. He was finished with running from his feelings and his desires. He wanted a home and family with Cain. Thanks to Bianca, they had an early start on the family, but Mal wasn't worried. He wasn't alone in this.

A cool spring breeze blew through the new leaves only now sprouting on the oaks and maples filling the forest next to the house. The air was damp and cold, slowly heating as the ice of winter melted. Another week, and it would be warm enough to start foraging for mushrooms.

Three more weeks, and he could likely start planting his spring garden full of broccoli, lettuce, greens, leeks, chives, and onions. He planned on planting herbs in May as well – ginger, lavender, basil, oregano, and as many more as he could think of. He had spent months researching what herbs, vegetables, and flowers to plant in central Maine and had a schedule for each month of the year now that he was home.

Mal frowned when he noticed the number of cars parked around the house. Cain knew he was arriving, so Mal thought for sure he would be alone. Months apart hadn't strained their relationship, but they needed time together. He still needed to introduce Cain to his family, and tell them all about Teddy's little sister. That was not a conversation Mal wanted to have. After Mal went on and on about how responsible he was, Grandpa David was going to enjoy teasing him about the unplanned pregnancy.

He parked and awkwardly climbed down from the truck. The baby had somehow managed to throw Mal's balance completely off. He waddled instead of striding, careful not to fall.

Cain waited for him on the front porch, face solemn, but eyes dancing with exhilaration. "You're home."

"I'm home," Mal said, grinning.

Cain was suddenly there in front of him, holding him close and pulling his face down for a kiss. The world disappeared and all Mal knew was the taste and feel of his man. For the first time in months, he felt safe and loved, warmth spreading through him. They had tried so hard to not let the distance get to them, but there was nothing so intimate as touching his lips to Cain's.

"You'll have time for that tonight," a laughing voice interrupted their kiss. "When we're all gone."

Mal frowned, pulling away from Cain. That voice sounded familiar.

Sure enough, Grandpa David stood in the doorway, smirking.

"What the fudge?" he asked, blinking several times to hopefully clear the blight on his vision.

"Nice to see you too." David pulled Mal away from Cain and hugged him tightly. "What's with the non-cursing. Boy, I taught you better."

"I've been watching *The Good Place* with Bianca, and well, I need to avoid cursing in front of the kids."

David patted Mal's extended abdomen. "Thought you could hide being pregnant, didn't you? We all watch your cooking videos, son. You're just lucky it's only the grandparents here."

Mal's eyes watered as he rubbed his face against his grandpa's shoulder. His familiar scent meant safety and love. He hadn't realized how much he had missed his grandpa.

"Did you talk to Gramps Wilson?"

"Yes, I did. His wife and he are here too. Hasn't told the rest of his family yet. We're going to have a family dinner and do it together."

His head shot up. "Wait. Grandpa Lucas is here?"

David scowled. "Yes, your favorite came too. All the grandparents are here, even Kat and Paul." He looked at Cain. "Those are his mother's parents."

One of Cain's eyebrows shot up. "Mal, I thought you said they were the normal ones?"

"Oh, no." Mal made a face. "Did they bring more taxidermy squirrels?"

"More?" Cain looked worried. "There are more? They brought three. One each for Teddy, the baby, and me."

"I have seven in storage," Mal admitted, smiling brightly. "After retiring, Grandpa Paul started gardening and squirrels became his enemies. He collects squirrels now and puts them in his garden. Says they warn the live squirrels of what will happen if they get his vegetables."

Cain's eyes narrowed. "That doesn't explain why they're wearing knitted costumes."

"Grandma Kat took up knitting when she retired."

"Dear God." Cain rubbed his hands down his face. "Here I thought you were a little weird, but it's really your whole family."

The phone rang and Mal answered it, still laughing. "Hey Van. You should bring Teddy and Bianca here. My grandparents are here and –"

"Mal," Van said, sobbing. "Bianca went to the police station. She turned herself in for murder."

CHAPTER 15

Cain handed Truffle to Gramps Wilson and let Betty out of the truck. The Kunekune followed them back to the house.

"Thanks. I'm not sure how long this will take." Cain fought panic as he thought of Bianca, alone and scared at the police station. It was one thing to tell himself she would be his daughter one day and another to feel the unexpected fear of a parent for their child. He hadn't realized the relationship had grown to that degree. Now he knew.

"We'll have her out in a few hours," John said. Cain's dad watched him, eyes bright with worry. "You love that kid. Don't you?"

Cain nodded. "She's my daughter. I don't know what happened, but I know her well enough to say that if she killed someone, it was either an accident or in self-defense."

Susan knelt down and fed a bit of broccoli to Betty. "I called Jasper a moment ago. He is on his way here."

They all startled when Mal whistled at them from his truck. "Super Bensons unite! Come on. We have a teenager to save. You too, Susan."

Cain's mom stood, eyes widening. "Me?" She pointed at herself.

"You have a comforting presence and a way of putting others at ease. My Bia may need that. Van and I are a mental mess right now."

"We haven't even properly met. How do you know all of that?" Susan jogged to the truck and got inside.

"Uh, reasons." Mal winced.

Cain sighed and pulled his dad to the truck. "We will be back soon. Thank you, Gramps."

The old man grinned. "It's a fine thing to see the last Benson all twisted up with love. Remember, Sheriff McKenzie is a good man. You can trust him to do right by Ms. Bianca."

Cain nodded and opened the driver's door. "Get over. You are not driving there."

"Why not?" Mal asked, hands shaking and a wild look in his eyes.

Cain helped Mal climb awkwardly over the console. "Buckle up." He looked in the backseat. His parents watched him with intense interest. "What a way to meet your future son-in-law and granddaughter."

John shrugged. "It doesn't involve costumes like meeting Carter's Elijah did."

"Costumes?" Mal asked.

"Star Wars themed wedding." Cain backed out of the drive and sped toward town.

Mal's foot tapped the floor like an over-anxious rabbit. "Themed wedding, huh? I would have liked to see that. Hey, if we get married, we should do a D&D themed wedding. Wouldn't that be something?"

Susan's reflection in the rearview mirror looked pained. "I will start looking for costumes. Any suggestions?"

"Elf druid and a cat warrior. Long black and white fur for the cat." Cain took a breath. "Bianca will be alright."

"I thought she was doing better." Mal looked close to tears. "She was so sad and scared when we first left, but time and therapy seemed to help. I don't know what is going on, and it bothers me."

Susan rested a hand on Mal's shoulder. "Children have a way of hiding the worse from their parents. She will explain when you see you, I'm sure."

Cain parked outside the police station, and they all hurried inside. Van stood at the front desk, pacing with a small infant in her arms. Cain froze in place, eyes widening.

Mal hugged her and the baby. "It's okay, Van. I brought the lawyers."

John stepped up. "Do you know the situation and exactly what she's said? She has to have an adult present to be properly questioned."

Cain stared at the baby. Curly brown hair topped it's head and curious green eyes watched him. *It's Teddy.*

Mal noticed his silence and watched him, eyes softening. "Do you want to hold our son?"

Cain nodded.

Van snorted and handed the baby to Cain. "You look like a dork right now." She looked a mess herself. "All I know is Bianca didn't want Teddy to see her in there, but she's confessed to killing Eugene Scott."

"Who the fudge is that?" Mal asked.

Suddenly scared out of his mind, Cain tuned them out and rocked his son. Teddy was so tiny. Cain and Mal were responsible for this small human. He thought back to the plants in his apartment in Atlanta. His cleaning lady took care of them. Otherwise, they would have died long ago.

Susan hugged him, eyes watering as she watched him. "You have a son and a daughter, Cain."

"I do." His laugh sounded a little wet. "Will you watch him, Mom?"

"I would be honored." She leaned up and kissed his cheek. "I will be right here if Bianca needs me."

"Eugene Scott's body was found back in October," John explained to Mal. "He murdered his wife in August and disappeared."

"He was her boss at the grocery store," Van said, nodding. "He was also the married man that got Bianca pregnant."

"Wait, he was in his forties." Mal's face turned a bright shade of red. "That fucker manipulated a teenage girl into having sex with him. I'm going to kill him."

"Already dead, dipshit." Van nudged his shoulder. "Let's go see Bianca."

Susan held Teddy and sat in one of the chairs near the door. "Dean is on his way too. I'll take Teddy to his house and come back." She looked at Mal. "He is a good friend of mine and can be trusted with your son. The Wilsons know him as well if that helps any."

"Oh, I know." Mal grinned. "He's my confidential informant on the Wilsons. He loves helping me plan my pranks."

Cain snorted a laugh. "Of course he does. It really is always the quiet ones."

With the issue of Teddy settled, they hurried to the sheriff's office. The station wasn't as bare and institutionalized as many of the police stations he had visited. The walls were tan and had pictures of police officers and community awards on the walls. The building was old, so it had scoffed hard wood floors that squeaked in places as they walked.

Bianca sat in a padded chair across from Sheriff McKenzie's desk. She was wrapped in a warm blanket and had a cup of steaming cocoa in her hands. Roe, Cain's friend, sat next to her, a comforting hand on her arm.

Her lips trembled when she saw them. "I'm sorry, Mal,

but you were right. Being an adult means taking responsibility for your actions. I couldn't just plan my life while a person's death hung over me."

"What has she said?" John's eyes narrowed on Sheriff McKenzie. "She is still considered a minor and should have a guardian present to be formally questioned."

The sheriff arched a brow and leaned back in his seat. "Bianca, do you want to tell them what you just told me?"

She nodded and took a deep breath. "The night Mal and I left Hobson Hills, well earlier that evening, I got a call from Eugene." She closed her eyes. "He was my boyfriend, but had broken up with me a few weeks earlier when I told him I was pregnant."

Mal's eye twitched, and Cain grabbed his hand. "Steady," he whispered.

"That night, he said he was sorry and asked me to meet him in our spot. I went to the clearing behind Farm Fresh. He was there, but he was… he was covered in –" she stopped, face full of fright. "He was covered in blood. I asked him what happened, and he told me his wife died, so we could be together if we left right then." She started shaking. "I knew that wasn't his blood. I knew it, so I turned and ran, but he caught me."

Mal and Van knelt on each side of her. Cain stood behind her, hand on her shoulder. He hated this. She never should have been in that kind of situation.

"He had a gun," she said, starting to sob. "He hit me with it and told me to be still. He said that she was dead, so we were leaving town right then." Bianca shook her head. "I didn't want to go, but he didn't care. I struggled and he wrapped his hands around my neck." She opened her eyes and took two deep breaths. "I kneed him in the groin, and he let me go, but he pointed the gun at me. I ran." She swallowed hard. "Two shots. He fired two shots at me, but it was getting dark. I got into his car and locked the doors. He shot at me, so I started the car. I thought it was in reverse, but it wasn't."

"It's okay," Mal whispered, patting her leg. "You're alright now."

"I drove into him," she admitted softly. "He bounced off the car like in the movies. It was horrible. I looked in the mirror and he was on the ground. I drove off." Her shoulders shook. "I just drove off and left him there. Dead."

"This is a clear case of self-defense," John said, crossing his arms over his chest. "The man had just murdered his own wife and threatened to kill Bianca."

"I agree," the sheriff nodded. "She was completely justified in her actions. However, she didn't drive to the police station. She drove home and left town."

"I didn't want to have the baby in jail." Bianca cried harder. "I murdered a person. Teddy shouldn't have to be part of that."

Sheriff McKenzie sighed. "You wouldn't have gone to jail. Bianca, Eugene Scott didn't die from being hit with a car."

"Care to explain?" Cain asked, arching a brow.

"He wasn't dead?" Bianca asked, voice small and hopeful.

Sheriff McKenzie shook his head. "I can't tell you how he died, but it wasn't by being hit by the car. He did have a couple of broken ribs and bruising, and his car also had damage, so we knew he had been hit, just not by who."

Bianca melted into her chair, her relief palpable. "I didn't kill him. Oh, God. I didn't kill him."

The door slammed open and Paula ran inside. "Wait! Bianca didn't kill Eugene Scott. I did."

Sherriff McKenzie sighed, and Roe stood up, waving Paula to his seat.

"Sit down and wait for your dad," Cain said, patting Bianca's shoulder to keep her in her seat. "Then you can tell us what happened."

CHAPTER 16

*H*ours later, Mal slid into the booth at Zoe's bakery, Honey Buns. "I want coffee and pastries right now."

"You can have a sip of my coffee, weirdo." Cain kissed the top of his head. "How about orange juice?"

"And herbal tea," Mal negotiated. "Plus the pastries."

"Done."

John had stayed behind with Van, Mark, and the girls. Jasper would arrive in a few hours to help out. There would be no trials since the girls had confessed, only sentencings. The sheriff and, surprisingly, the county prosecutor had both promised to talk to the judge and put in a good word for the teens. They wanted it to done and over, for the girls and for the town. Eugene Scott had done some horrible things.

Paula had killed Eugene Scott. She had shot him with his own gun. After he assaulted Bianca, Paula comforted her, then agreed to go back to the clearing to find Bianca's phone. According to Paula, Eugene was there, stumbling around and angry. He yelled at Paula and ran toward her. Paula had told them how she picked up his gun and closed her eyes before firing toward him. She had hit him straight in the chest. After that, the teen had run away, dropping the gun in the process.

Sheriff McKenzie had told them Paula's version of events matched up with the evidence. The county prosecutor had agreed that there was ample evidence of self-defense, so he had chosen not to pursue manslaughter charges. The only problem now was that both girls had not gone to the police.

"Those girls." Mal groaned and rubbed his eyes. They should have gone straight to Sheriff McKenzie. If not that, then Van should have made Bianca go to the police when they found her beaten and bruised. Paula would have never gone back to the clearing, and fucking Eugene Scott would be rotting in a jail cell. Hell, if he was passing out blame, then he needed to acknowledge that he should have asked more questions.

"Would of, should of," he mumbled, fighting a yawn. Now, both teenagers faced the charge of obstruction of justice. Yes, it was better than manslaughter, but it could still be a felony if the judge decided it was.

"Did you hear about those girls that killed Eugene Scott?" an older woman asked her companion at the table next to his. "What is wrong with the younger generation now-a-days?"

Mal growled, ready to yell at the gossips.

"Enough of that," Zoe told them, refilling their drinks. "We don't know the whole story. What we do know is that Eugene was a bastard."

"Well, that's true," the woman said, patting her mouth with a napkin. "It's just so shocking."

"Violence always is." Zoe looked sad. "Those poor girls are probably a mess right now. They did the right thing in confessing, but I bet they're scared."

The elderly woman winced, looking slightly guilty. "I

should make a casserole for their families. I bet they don't have the time or energy to stay fed."

"Good idea." Zoe smiled. "I believe I'll bring coffee and breakfast sandwiches to the station right now. I hear they've been there all night."

Mal sniffled. All it took sometimes was one person deciding not to fuel hateful gossip. Bianca and Paula didn't need the town's gossips speculating about them. He was glad he had only pranked Zoe twice over the years. She was good people.

Cain sat down with their food, and Zoe turned to smile at them. "Is this the man I've been hearing all about, Cain?"

Cain yawned. "Meet Mal. Mal, this is Zoe. Wait, I'm sure you already know about her."

"Zoe owns the bakery and is married to Gib. She's the granddaughter of Gramps Wilson, the daughter of Barry and Jamie, and the sister of Abel and Ernie. She likes martinis and has a pet rabbit." Mal sighed. "That's all I really know. I need to give her more of my time. She deserves custom designed pranks."

Her eyes narrowed. "You're the one that posed ginger-bread cookies in my kitchen." She glared at him. "Did you have to have them decapitating one of their own? It was disturbing, especially the girl cookie crying over the headless body."

"Generic." Mal shook his head, slightly embarrassed. "If I knew more about you, I could have done so much better."

"You're as bad as my brothers." She rolled her eyes and walked away."

Joy built as Mal brushed tears from his eyes. "Did you hear that? She sees me as family already. I can't wait for Grandpa David and Gramps Wilson to make the announcement."

Cain watched him, eyes darkening. "I love you so much."

The buzz of people filling the bakery disappeared until only the alpha of his heart was there. "I love you too. Are you sure about doing this? It's not too late for you to duck out."

Cain snorted a laugh. "It is way too late for that. You already have my heart. There is no possibility of me leaving now."

"What if Jasper dumped his alpha and wanted to be with you?"

"Too late. I have you and there is absolutely no one better."

"Hmm." Mal felt inordinately happy to hear him say that. He thought he had gotten over those doubts months ago. "What about the kids? It would be overwhelming for anyone." Mal patted his extended baby bump. "You only have responsibility toward one of the three kids I come with."

"Sorry, but I already love Bianca and Teddy too." He shook his head. "Besides, what would Uncle Ron think of me if I didn't love all the kids?"

"This is true." Mal reached for his hand. "You're really sure?"

"One hundred percent." Cain watched him for a moment. "Are you sure? I'm not like your first love. Rick is fun and easy-going."

Mal shook his head, fighting a smile. No, Cain wasn't like Rick, and the love he felt for his alpha was different than the unrequited painful love that had sent Mal running after graduation. Love that was returned was so much better. It felt like a circle of fondness, care, and adoration, ever cycling between them. He loved Cain's serious nature as much as he loved his willingness to follow Mal into trouble.

The way he made Mal feel about himself was just as important. Mal had three kids now. The responsibility would have sent past him into spirals. Now, he was scared, but determined. That was because Cain hadn't even hesitated to believe in him. He hadn't told Mal that he wasn't ready for a child. He hadn't pointed out that Mal still lived a nomadic life in an RV. He had only shrugged and said alright. If it was what Mal wanted, then it would happen.

"I want to live the rest of my life with you by my side," Mal told Cain. "Maybe we didn't have a traditional start to our relationship, but that's just how the Reeds do things."

Cain moved over to his side of the booth and pulled Mal into his arms. "Our love story is a damn good one to add to the Reed family history."

"It is." Mal settled his head on top of Cain's.

They stayed in each other's arms while they ate their breakfast and fought yawns. An hour later, John slid in front of them, looking ten years younger.

"Jasper arrived early," he told them, grinning. "The sheriff pulled some strings to get the judge there immediately. Thirty minutes with them both, and the girls were sentenced to a year of community service. They have to remain in Maine during that time, but otherwise, they are free to return home and be the kids they are meant to be."

Mal whooped loudly, startling the other customers. Then he leaned against Cain and closed his eyes. "Just a little nap, then we'll go get Teddy and the critters. Just ten minutes, okay?"

HOURS LATER, Mal woke to the sound of pages slowly turning. He lay in the most comfortable bed he had ever been in. The cool sheets were light gray, and the fluffy comforter was a calm pattern of blue, white and gray stripes. The bed itself was large, easily a California king size.

Best of all was the purring bundle of fur tucked against his abdomen. Truffle enjoyed communing with the monster baby, and Mal would never object because the purring always calmed the baby.

Mal sniffed, then rubbed his eyes before sitting up. Even though he had never been there, he knew that he was in the new room he would share with Cain. The walls were a faint greyish white while the furniture was handmade of white oak. *Harper's work,* he thought, smiling. The room was big with a large window seat. Next to the window seat were two very comfortable looking reading chairs.

He smiled at the man sitting with a book in one of those chairs. "Grandpa Lucas."

Lucas looked up, brown face brightening when his dark eyes fell on Mal. "You're finally awake, son. You didn't even rouse when that alpha of yours carried you in here."

Mal shifted and climbed out of bed, careful not to disturb Truffle. "I don't even remember getting home. Having kids is hard, Grandpa Lucas."

The large man stood and pulled him into a hug. "It really is. You started with a teenager too. That's even worse." Lucas gave him a mischievous look. "You look really happy, Mal. Tired, yes, but also happy."

Mal stretched his body and grinned. "That would be because of Cain. Have you met him?"

Lucas nodded and gently settled Mal into a chair before draping a soft, knitted blanket over him. "I have." He sat in the other chair, looking delighted. "I have to say I was expecting another Rick, but your Cain is very different. He has such a calm presence and serious demeanor. He hasn't let anyone else hold Teddy since everyone arrived home."

Grandpa Lucas was the only one in the family that knew about Mal's feelings for Rick. He knew all of Mal's secrets.

"Don't let Cain fool you." Mal smirked. "He helps me with my pranks all the time."

Lucas chuckled. "I don't know if you should be proud of

that or not. Oh, you wouldn't know yet, but the Wilsons are all here. David, Vivi, Addy, and Laurel cooked a large amount of food. Paul, Kat, and I set up picnic tables in the backyard since it isn't raining. Take a look."

Mal peeked outside. The large backyard was partially shaded by two large oak trees and gently sloped down to the lake. Normally, it was rather bare, but now, it had several picnic tables, a buffet table covered with food, and a lot of Wilsons. Each of Gerard and Laurel Wilson's children were there with their spouses and grandchildren. The grandchildren had in turn brought their own partners and children. It was a very full backyard.

Fairy lights twinkled in the trees and small candles and a pretty, elaborately decorated box lay center on each of the picnic tables. He smiled when he saw Betty trotting in and out of the crowd, begging for food. Van and Mark were even there, cuddled together at one of the tables.

The door opened and Susan peeked inside. "You are awake. Good timing, dear." The lovely blond was perfectly put together in designer clothes and tasteful makeup.

Mal grinned, thinking of how he would appear next to her in his ripped jeans, oversized flannel shirt, and flip flops. His hair was a mess too, likely standing up in places it shouldn't. He couldn't say he minded, though. Cain liked him just as he was, be it in his sexy clothes or hiking clothes.

Susan answered his grin with one of her own. "Oh, Mal. When Cain first told us about you, I was worried that the two of you were moving too fast. However, now that I have seen you together, I could not be happier."

Lucas stood and smoothed down Mal's hair. "I empathize, Susan. They have certainly moved quickly, but the Reed family tends to do that."

She laughed. "So do the Bensons."

"Is he awake?" Dean came in the room, smiling when he

saw Mal. "Thank you for trusting me with Teddy last night, Mal. That is one sweet baby."

Mal nodded. "Truth, brother."

Susan pursed her lips. "I had almost forgotten you two know each other. I must say, Mal, I was not pleased to learn you were the one trying to steal my best friend."

Mal gasped dramatically, as he was often wont to do. "I would never steal Dean from you. I just coldly use him for information on the Wilsons for my pranks."

"And he sends Christmas and birthday presents each year," Dean added, smiling innocently. "We often meet for coffee and talk over prank ideas. Oh, and I didn't tell you this, Susan, but Mal and I went foraging for blackberries once too. Without you."

Susan's face scrunched up as she pouted. "Never again. You must always take me with you when you go for coffee or go foraging. Whatever that is."

"Traipsing through the woods looking for edible yummies," Lucas explained, amused.

She looked horrified and glared at Dean. "You tricked me. I told you several times now that I do not care for hiking."

"You committed now." Dean laughed and hugged her. "You'll survive. I promise."

"Oh, very well. She looked Mal up and down with a sigh. "You must be starving. Gramps and David are about to make an announcement. They wanted to wait until you were awake."

Mal's stomach rumbled. "I am so ready for food. Let's do this."

As he stood, Truffle launched himself to Mal's shoulder and draped himself across the omega. Together, they all went outside, joining the growing crowd of Wilsons.

"I will get you some food." Susan patted his arm and

guided him to a chair. I remember how much my feet hurt when I was pregnant."

Mal sighed. "I can't see my feet anymore. Do I even have any?"

"Two very swollen feet." Dean gave him a sweet look. "How do you like pregnancy?"

"It's horrible." Mal scowled. "Don't get me wrong, I love this kid growing inside me, but if Cain wants anymore children, then we're adopting. Teddy was much easier to deal with."

"Yes, because Bianca was the one pregnant with him." Lucas sat down next to him.

As if saying her name summoned her, Bianca and Paula both appeared at his side. Both carried a taxidermy squirrel.

"Grandpa Paul got to you, didn't he?" Mal asked.

"It means we're family." Paula shrugged. "It's nice."

"It's hideous," Bianca corrected her friend. "But if it makes him happy, then so be it. According to Grandma Addy, part of being in the Reed family is simply enduring."

Lucas looked thoughtful for a moment. "Yeah, that's accurate."

The two girls hugged Mal together. "How are you feeling?" Bianca asked.

"Like a swollen whale. How are you?"

"As light as air." She spun around, looking especially happy. "I'm so relieved everything is out in the open. I don't care if I have to clean roads for eternity."

Mal nodded, happy that the whole thing was over. He swallowed hard when he saw Cain walking toward him, a plate of food in his hands. Many of his sex dreams started this way. However, they didn't include the tiny infant balanced in one of Cain's arms.

Cain handed Mal the plate, then sat beside him. "How are you, love?"

Before he could answer, Bianca grabbed the cake off of his plate. "No cake for you. Too much sugar isn't good for pregnant people." She smirked. "That's what you told me all the time anyway. Are those potatoes and rolls? Too many carbs aren't good for baby," she sing-songed.

Mal frowned. "Pregnancy was much easier to deal with when it was you that I could boss around."

Bianca snorted. "You enjoyed it far too much. Here, you can have a little bit of the cake but give me that roll."

"It's one of Grammy Wilson's rolls," he said, whining.

"Cake or roll?" Bianca asked, arching a brow in a surprisingly accurate impersonation of Cain.

"Cake," he said with a sigh.

She nodded. "Okay. Cain, I'll email you the pregnancy rules he gave me for the last trimester. Make him stick to it, even when he doesn't want to. They do actually help."

Cain gave him a nervous look. "He tried to bite me when I told him he shouldn't have any more pastries yesterday."

"Stay strong, my man." Paula patted Cain's shoulder. "Stay strong."

Mal started eating as Grandpa David and Gramps climbed atop one of the tables. He vaguely wondered if that was a good idea considering how old they were.

"Can I have your attention, please?" Gramps called out. "I have some news to share."

Everyone quieted down and turned to look at Gramps and David.

Gramps cleared his throat, looking nervous. "My fathers were an alpha and omega couple, and I loved them both very much. They were good parents, and I wish every day that all of you could have met them. The same with my younger brother. He would have loved knowing all of you. No one from my childhood family is alive anymore, and I miss them." Gramps' eyes glistened with tears. "Siblings are a treasure, and I always wanted more of them."

Mal looked over the Wilson clan as he ate, noting the nods coming from most of them. The Wilsons were a prolific bunch and knew the value of having the support of a large family.

"With that in mind, I would like to tell you a story about my omega father," Gramps continued. "He was an omega who lived in a world where loving men and women equally was a sin. Dad hid his desires as much as he could, and his family pressured him to only date alphas because, according to them, that's what God wanted."

Clearly the crowd of Wilsons didn't agree if their frowns had anything to say.

"Dad never felt comfortable with himself. He believed his desires were wrong and tried to ignore his interest in women. Then he met a woman named Grace. She taught him to accept himself for who he was. Though they didn't love one another, they were good friends and spent one night together. Not long after, Dad met an alpha and fell in love. His family was happy, but that no longer mattered to him. All that mattered was that he was true to himself. Shortly after the wedding, he heard that his good friend, Grace, had passed away. My alpha father and he decided that if they ever had a daughter, they would name her Grace in remembrance of the friend that taught the omega so much."

"Grace," Cain whispered, looking fascinated. "I really like that name."

Mal set his plate down and took Cain's hand, smiling. "I do too."

Gramps continued his story. "My fathers went on to live a full life and taught their own sons the importance of accepting one another's differences. They never had that daughter, but they never forgot about Grace."

David shared a nervous smile with Gramps. "I'm David Reed. My mother's name was Grace. She got pregnant with me from a night spent with a good friend. She never told that friend about me because he had fallen in love and gotten married."

Mal's eyes watered as he watched each of the Wilsons making the connection between David and Gramps.

"I have another brother," Gramps said, crying as he laughed. He slung an arm around David. "He has a large family of his on in Washington state. How about that, right? It's not everyday you discover you have more family than you thought." He waved toward Mal. "That young man over there with Cain is Malcolm Reed, named after my omega father. Cain you believe it?"

As one, his Wilson cousins stared at him and smiled evilly. "Our new cousin was the one pranking us over the years?" Zoe asked.

"Not all of the pranks," Mal said, taking another bite of his mashed potatoes. "You all prank each other a lot. You can't blame me for everything."

"Oh, but we can," Ernie said, cackling. "We have a new cousin to torment."

The younger generations of Wilsons cheered, clearly happy with Mal's existence. Their parents were still wiping their eyes and saying hello to David. Mal didn't want to even think about what they would say.

"What have I done?" he asked Cain, cuddling up to his alpha. "Do you think they'll prank me back?"

"Yes," Cain answered with a grin. "And you'll deserve every bit of it."

Grandpa Lucas chuckled and pulled his phone out. "Let's start this right." He pushed a button and all the small boxes at the center of the tables burst open, shooting glitter and confetti everywhere.

"Damn it," Marco Wilson said, the large cowboy covered in pink glitter. "This better come off in the shower."

Mal laughed. "I love you, Grandpa Lucas."

"It's always the quiet ones." Cain sighed and hugged Mal closer. "Always."

A few months later, the summer breeze made the trees beside around them sway as the scent of pine and lilacs swirled. It was a good day for a wedding. Mal's grandparents and Cain's mom had gone all out with the decorations. From the hand-carved wooden wedding arch to the dragon topped wedding cake, everything followed a D&D theme.

Cain stood in front of his friends and family, dressed in chainmail and fuzzy cat ears. He held Teddy in one arm, the little boy dressed as a calico kitten. Across from him, stood Mal, the most beautiful elvan druid in a long green robe. He held an equally beautiful little girl dressed as a black and white kitten. Their daughter, Grace, was only two months old, but they couldn't possibly get married without her.

Bianca, Van, and Rick stood to one side of them and Roe and Cain's brothers stood on the other. Each wore their own costumes. Bianca and Roe were dressed as elves, with pointy ears and long robes. Van and Carter were in chainmail and dressed as orcs, green skin and tusks included. Rick was a bit shorter than everyone else and had dressed as a halfling.

Caden was the only human and was dressed in leather archer's armor.

Their friends and family wore their own costumes ranging from traditional medieval garb to orc and elf costumes. There were well over three hundred there for the wedding. A surprising number of Reeds had flown to Maine, and many of Cain and Mal's friends had travelled in from out of state.

All of that was simply icing on the cake. The true magic was the man that stood with him. Mal was his weird, wonderful omega, and Cain wanted to live every moment of the rest of his life with him.

AUTHOR'S NOTE

If you would like to keep up with releases, I have a Patreon account: patreon.com/cwgrayauthor. You may also like and follow me on Instagram (@c.w._gray) or Facebook (@cwgrayauthor). I would love for you to join C.W. Gray's Reading Nook on Facebook. It's a relaxing, fun group. You can also visit my website at https://cwgray-author.com.

Writing as Chloe Gray

- A Little Bit of Perfect – contemporary, non-mpreg, Daddy/Little age play

Writing as C.W. Gray

- **Charybdis Station Chronicles** – *science fiction/fantasy, mpreg*

The Blue Solace Series
Charybdis Station
The Crellic Revival

- The Hobson Hills Omegas – non-shifter, mpreg, omegaverse
- Holiday Omegas Shorts – holiday short stories from the world of The Silver Isles – paranormal, mpreg, omegaverse

- The Silver Isles – paranormal, mermen, mpreg, omegaverse

142